Lucas stiffened. Something was wrong.

Charlotte gasped for a breath, her fingernails digging into his palm. "Help..."

He cradled her hand between both of his, soothing her. "You're safe now, Charlotte. You're in the hospital and you're safe." But those four teenagers weren't.

She pushed at the sheets and grabbed the bed rail with her free hand. "I...can't see," she whispered between choked breaths. "I can't see you. I can't see anything."

Lucas's pulse clamored. "You mean you can't see the shooter? You were in the studio, weren't you? Or did you and the girls hide?"

"No...I was there," she cried, her chest heaving. "They stormed in and took them. I tried to save them, but the big one shot me and hit me in the head."

He leaned over the bed and stroked her arm. "Charlotte, it's okay, I know it was terrifying and you wanted to save your students. Just tell me what you saw and we can still save them."

"You don't understand. I can't see. Anything."

SAFE AT HAWK'S LANDING

USA TODAY Bestselling Author

RITA HERRON

To my beautiful daughter Elizabeth—who works tirelessly to help victims of domestic violence and prevent human trafficking

So proud of you!

Love you always, Mom

ISBN-13: 978-1-335-52611-3

Safe at Hawk's Landing

Copyright © 2017 by Rita B. Herron

PLEASE RECYCLE

THIS PRODUCT IS RECYCLABLE

Recycling programs for this product may not exist in your area.

For questions and comments about the quality of this book, please contact us at CustomerService@Harlequin.com.

Printed in U.S.A.

HARLEQUIN®

™ www.Harlequin.com

USA TODAY bestselling author **Rita Herron** wrote her first book when she was twelve but didn't think real people grew up to be writers. Now she writes so she doesn't have to get a real job. A former kindergarten teacher and workshop leader, she traded storytelling to kids for writing romance, and now she writes romantic comedies and romantic suspense. Rita lives in Georgia with her family. She loves to hear from readers, so please visit her website, ritaherron.com.

Books by Rita Herron

Harlequin Intrigue

Badge of Justice

Redemption at Hawk's Landing
Safe at Hawk's Landing

The Heroes of Horseshoe Creek

Lock, Stock and McCullen
McCullen's Secret Son
Roping Ray McCullen
Warrior Son
The Missing McCullen
The Last McCullen

Bucking Bronc Lodge

Certified Cowboy
Cowboy in the Extreme
Cowboy to the Max
Cowboy Cop
Native Cowboy
Ultimate Cowboy

Cold Case at Camden Crossing
Cold Case at Carlton's Canyon
Cold Case at Cobra Creek
Cold Case in Cherokee Crossing

Visit the Author Profile page at Harlequin.com.

CAST OF CHARACTERS

Special Agent Lucas Hawk—He will do anything to stop the human-trafficking ring targeting Texas—and to protect Charlotte Reacher, the only surviving witness to the men's crimes.

Charlotte Reacher—Blinded by the men who kidnapped four students in her therapeutic art class, she must accept Lucas's help and his protection in order to save the girls. But can she resist the sizzling attraction she feels for Lucas?

Evie Cranton—She shot one of her foster fathers when he tried to molest her. Could he have sold her out to the trafficking ring to get revenge?

Herman Stanley—This banker has made a fortune off swindling people out of their property—has he also been selling and buying girls into sex slavery?

Stefan Ludwig—Is he the head of the trafficking ring?

Earl Ramus—Lucas killed him to protect Charlotte. But dead men can't talk—can they?

Geoffrey Williams—Could this city councilman be involved in the human-trafficking ring?

Louise Summerton—Her parents thought she ran away with a boy she met online. Was the meeting a setup to lure her into the hands of the trafficking ring?

Chapter One

Charlotte Reacher knew what it was like to be alone. Without a home or family.

Unwanted. Unloved.

That loneliness had inspired her to start her art program for teenage girls in Tumbleweed, Texas. This particular group of four were all foster kids and needed reassurance and love.

She strolled through the studio smiling at the girls perched behind canvases that had once been blank slates, but now were being transformed. When they'd first organized the group six weeks ago, most of them had painted drab, colorless pictures, all grays and blacks, depicting the despair in their lives.

Not every girl had a bikini body, liked makeup and glamour magazines or cheerleading.

And not every girl had parents with the money to fix her flaws.

The confident ones knew how to socialize, make friends and express themselves, while others wilted on the inside, withdrew and suffered from low self-esteem. Cruel classmates complicated the situation with teasing and bullying, and caused the girls to die a little with every mean word said.

It had been the same for her, growing up in the system. Her port-wine birthmark had drawn cruel remarks and stares, killing her own confidence.

She brushed her fingers over her cheek. Thanks to a gifted and generous plastic surgeon, who'd offered her services to needy kids when Charlotte was eleven, the skin was smooth now, the birthmark gone.

Still, the internal scars remained. These girls had scars, too. Both physical and emotional.

But here—in her studio, Expressions—everyone was free to paint or draw whatever they wanted with no judgment.

She just hoped the small town of Tumbleweed embraced the teens. So far, the locals had been nice to her. She'd made friends with Honey Granger Hawk, the developer who'd built the small house she lived in. Honey appreciated her cause and had thrown in the studio renovation for next to nothing.

Now Charlotte had a home, a friend and a business. And hopefully a family in this town and her students…

She adjusted the volume of the music playing in the background. Early on, she'd discovered that music relaxed her and the students. Now she allowed the girls to select the CDs they wanted to listen to during their sessions. Today Evie had chosen an upbeat country song.

"Ms. Charlotte, what do you think?" Fifteen-year-old Mae Lynn looked up at her with a mixture of apprehension and hope. She was shy and the most fragile of all of them, but she'd begun to warm up.

"I like the way you've used the colors," Charlotte said. It was obvious the sea of blues and grays represented her changing mood swings. Who could blame her, though? The poor kid had been in and out of more than ten homes in five years.

Two girls who were horse lovers, sixteen-year-old Agnes and her fourteen-year-old sister, Adrian, chatted softly about their portrayals of a big ranch where they hoped to live one day, while thirteen-year-old Evie splashed pinks and blues and purples in a whimsical pattern. Despite the fact that she'd ended up in a group home, Evie had a perpetually positive attitude.

Hopefully, her attitude would rub off on the others.

Suddenly, the front door to the studio opened, and Charlotte glanced up, hoping to see Sally, another foster child she'd invited to the class, but instead four tall masked men dressed in black stormed in, guns raised and aimed at the girls.

Charlotte froze, mentally assessing the situation. She had to protect her students no matter what. Pulse hammering, she stepped forward, placing herself between the men and girls.

The biggest man turned the gun on her. "Don't move."

She stared at the snake tattoo, then noticed a bolt of lightning tattooed on his neck.

Behind her, the girls screamed. Charlotte raised her hands in a submissive gesture. "Please don't hurt them," she said in a choked voice. "I don't keep much money here, but you can take it all."

"We don't want your money," the shortest guy shouted. "Get on the ground."

A sob echoed behind her, then another scream.

"I said get down!" the one who seemed to be in charge barked.

Charlotte dropped to the floor, her gaze scanning the

room for something to use as a weapon, but her art supplies and brushes wouldn't do any good against these guns. Semiautomatics. They weren't playing around.

Her phone was inside her purse in her office, too. She didn't have a weapon or an alarm.

Boots clicked on the wood floor as the heaviest man strode to her. With one quick grunt, he slammed the butt of the gun against her head. Stars swam in front of her eyes as the world spun. More screams rent the air, shrill and piercing.

Panic shot through Charlotte. She had to do something. If the men didn't want money, what did they want?

"Leave us alone!" Adrian cried.

"Don't shoot!" Agnes said shakily.

A bullet pinged off the ceiling, silencing them all.

Evie ducked behind an easel while the sisters hunched together beneath a table. Mae Lynn pushed her easel over, paint splattering, and ran for the door, but one of the men grabbed her as if she weighed nothing.

"Please don't hurt me," Mae Lynn cried.

Charlotte pushed to her hands and knees, desperate. "Let her go. Take me if you want, but leave these kids alone."

A bark of sarcastic laughter, sickening in its sound, filled the air as the brute slammed the gun against her head again, then jerked her arm and flung her against the wall. Pain ricocheted through her head and shoulder and, for a second, she thought she might pass out.

Then everything happened at once.

The men charged the girls. Agnes and Adrian kicked and fought. Mae Lynn was sobbing, trying to wrestle free, while Evie scrambled toward the back room to escape, throwing chairs and paintbrushes, whatever she could grasp hold of.

The man chasing Evie tossed the table aside, then snatched her up, laughing as she flailed and fought.

One of them muttered something, but she couldn't understand the words.

Then the men dragged the girls toward the door to the outside. Charlotte couldn't let them get away.

Ignoring the pain in her skull, she grabbed the wall and pulled herself up, then staggered forward.

A second later, a gunshot erupted, then pain scared her shoulder where the bullet had struck. Another bullet zinged by her head and skimmed her temple, and her legs gave way.

She collapsed on the floor, blood gushing from her shoulder. "Let them go!" She crawled after them, but another bullet pinged the floor in front of her, then the intruders dragged the girls through the door.

The biggest brute stood guard, his gun releasing more ammunition across the room to keep her at bay. Bullets pierced the walls and ripped at the canvases, sending paint tubes and containers spilling to the floor.

Her blood mingled with the paint, and the two blended together, the vibrant colors fading to a dull brown. The huge man strode to her and slammed the gun against her head one more time.

A sharp pain splintered her skull, then the world turned black as he disappeared out the door.

SPECIAL AGENT LUCAS HAWK studied the photographs of the missing girls from Waco and Abilene on the white board in the task-force meeting room.

Two kidnappings, two different cities in Texas. Both

by a group of masked men who'd abducted teenagers. Female teenagers.

The men's motive hadn't been confirmed, but Lucas suspected what they were doing, and it made him sick to his stomach.

He'd lost his own sister when she was just a kid and he'd been fifteen, and understood the agony these families must be suffering.

"There are eleven victims in Texas so far," Special Agent Tradd Hoover stated.

So far? Implying he believed there would be more.

"At this point, none of the victims have been found. We have no real lead as to where the men are holding the girls, either." Agent Hoover paused, his expression grim. "Or for how long."

The sheriff from Waco raised his hand. "You don't think they're killing them?"

Agent Hoover shook his head. "If they were, we would have found bodies. We believe this is a highly organized human-trafficking ring. They're bold, aggressive, and the fact that they're abducting groups of teens implies they have orders to fill."

"Any witnesses?" Lucas asked.

"None that have survived," Agent Hoover said. "The kidnappers come armed and dangerous, and have taken out anyone in their path."

The door opened, and Deputy Director Henry Fredericks stepped into the room, rubbing a hand over his bald head. "Just got a call. Another group kidnapping. Four victims." He flicked his pointer finger toward Lucas. "Your hometown, Hawk. Your brother called it in. He wants us there. Yesterday."

A coldness swept over Lucas. The trafficking ring had struck Tumbleweed.

For God's sake, they'd just finally closed the book on his sister's disappearance and death.

With four teenagers from Tumbleweed missing, the town would be in an uproar.

"You hear me, Special Agent Hawk?" the deputy director said.

Lucas jerked himself to attention and stood. "Yes, sir, I'm on my way."

The deputy director cleared his throat. "There's something else. This time there's a witness. She's been shot and needs surgery. But if she makes it, we may have caught a break and she can tell us more about these sons of bitches."

Lucas nodded. If she knew anything, he'd find out. Then hopefully they could stop this crew before they got too far away with the teens.

The wind whistled as he stepped outside. He jogged to his car and sped from the parking lot. The deputy director had said *if* the witness survived. He couldn't waste time.

He pressed Harrison's number as he drove, tension knotting his shoulders. His brother answered on the third ring.

"I'm on my way, Harrison. The deputy director said you have a witness."

"Hopefully," Harrison said. "She's unconscious now. The medics are transporting her to the hospital."

"How seriously is she hurt?"

"Took a bullet to the shoulder, lost a lot of blood. Looks like one of the jerks beat her in the head with the butt of a semi. Could be serious." Harrison's voice sounded gruff. "Her name's Charlotte Reacher, Lucas. She's a friend of Honey's."

Damn. "Where did it happen?"

"In town. Charlotte's art studio, Expressions. She does art therapy with troubled kids and adolescents."

The injustice of the situation made his blood boil. She sounded like a good woman. She sure as hell hadn't deserved this.

"All four of the teens were foster kids."

Lucas's gut clenched. Most crews slipped in quietly and worked under the radar. These bastards were practically shoving their crimes in the faces of the residents and the law.

They probably thought a small-town sheriff couldn't handle the challenge.

Big mistake. They didn't know his brother.

"We have to find them, Lucas," Harrison said. "This town is having a hard time with the recent arrest of one of our own. A violent attack like this is gonna hit hard."

His brother was right. Lucas tightened his hands around the steering wheel and pressed the accelerator.

Every second the girls were missing gave the kidnappers more time to get away.

AN HOUR LATER, Lucas parked in front of Expressions. Crime-scene tape had already been erected in front of the building and along the sidewalk outside, looking ominous against the soothing pale blue of the studio's exterior.

Harrison's deputy, Mitchell Bronson, was working to keep the growing crowd from crossing the line, but hushed whispers and worried, shocked looks floated through the group.

"I'm going to canvass the neighboring businesses and locals," Deputy Bronson said. "Sheriff said for you to go on in."

Lucas visually swept the street signs and posts. "Surveillance cameras?"

"Afraid not."

Damn, that would have helped. "Be sure to ask if anyone saw the getaway vehicle," Lucas said.

The deputy nodded and addressed the onlookers, holding his hands up to calm the crowd.

Lucas paused in the doorway to analyze the scene. The room was decorated with color palettes and paintings most likely done by students. A brightly lit sign showcasing the name sparkled in deep purple and yellow letters, at odds with the violence that had happened here today.

Worse, the room had been turned upside down in a scene that could only be described as chaotic. Tables, chairs, canvases and paint supplies were scattered across the room. Bullet holes marred the walls and canvases, as if more than one shooter had fired randomly across the space, hitting everything in sight.

Paint tubes, bottles and containers had spilled, the paint running together, converging on the light wood floors in an ugly brown smear.

Footprints in different sizes that must belong to the girls tracked the paint across the floor, indicating the victims had fought back, and that at least one of them had been dragged.

A female's cowboy boot lay in one corner, obviously lost during the struggle. Beads from a bracelet or necklace were scattered by a bin of paint smocks.

Bloody fingerprints dotted the floor and wall.

"Here's what I think happened," Harrison said. "According to the schedule posted in the teacher's office, Charlotte was conducting a class. Four students." Harrison gestured toward the door. "Looks like the kidnappers just walked in. No sign of forced entry. Door was probably unlocked." He pointed toward the pool of blood on the floor. "Owner of the coffee shop/bookstore next door said Charlotte was giving, kind and dedicated to her students." Harrison ran a hand through his hair, emotion thickening his voice. "Honey would agree to that. She liked what Charlotte was doing here so much that she renovated this space for her at cost."

Lucas clenched his hands into fists. "Have you told Honey yet?"

Harrison shook his head. "No. I'm not looking forward to it, either."

Lucas patted his brother's arm. "She's strong. Tough. She can handle it."

"I know, but I...want to protect that woman from everything bad."

The love in Harrison's voice twisted Lucas's insides. The Hawk brothers had all been loners. He'd never expected Harrison to marry. Then Honey came back to town...

Harrison gestured around the room. "Charlotte obviously tried to stop the men, but judging from the number of bullet holes, they were heavily armed and opened fire. While she was down, the men snatched the teenagers and kept firing to prevent Charlotte from following. She passed out on the floor in that pool of blood. My guess is they thought she was hit in the chest and would bleed to death."

Lucas's stomach squeezed at the sight of the bloody

fingerprints where the woman had crawled to the door. Even injured, she'd tried to save the girls.

"Any specifics on the hostages?" Lucas asked.

"Not yet. We're working on compiling that information."

"What about Charlotte? Any family?"

"No. She was alone. That's what drew her to Honey and these adolescents."

Damn. Lucas didn't know the woman, but he already admired her.

He just hoped she survived and could help them. Otherwise, the four teenagers might be lost forever.

Chapter Two

Pain throbbed through Charlotte's head and body. She tried to open her eyes, but a black void swirled around her and a heavy nothingness dragged her into its abyss.

Machines beeped. Low voices murmured. Metal clanged.

Where was she? What had happened?

"Got the bullet," a man said. "Need to stop the bleeding."

Charlotte searched her mind—she must be in surgery...but why?

A burning sensation seeped through her, followed by more darkness and quiet. Then a loud popping sound. Screams. Footsteps pounding. Her paints and canvases crashing.

Her studio, she was back there...the girls were painting, the music flowing, the door opened...

Terror seized her. Strange men stormed in. Men wearing masks. They were dressed in black.

And they had guns...

More screams. She had to save the girls...

The popping sound again. The bullet pierced her. Her head throbbed, colors bleeding together, fading.

Quiet again. Blissful quiet. Except for the voices. Someone touching her. A gentle hand.

"You're going to make it, Ms. Reacher," a woman said. "Just rest now."

Rest? The world twirled, nausea flooded her, then that slow burn again. She tried to move, but her limbs were heavy. Weighted. Something was attached to her arm. An IV.

"The police want to talk to you, but they'll have to wait. Sleep now."

Sleep? Rest? How could she? There was something she had to do. Something important.

The screams echoed in her head again. Her students…they needed her.

Terror and despair flooded her. Adrian, Agnes, Mae Lynn…sweet Evie…they were crying, sobbing, begging for help.

LUCAS PACED THE waiting room, anxious to talk to Charlotte Reacher.

Meanwhile, he phoned Tradd Hoover.

"The art teacher is still in surgery," he told Tradd. "The studio where the attack happened looked like a war zone. Bullet holes everywhere. My brother, Sheriff Harrison Hawk, is supervising the crime-scene unit."

"All four girls were foster kids?"

"That's right."

"That sucks," Tradd said. "As if their lives haven't already been hard enough." Tradd made a clicking sound with his teeth. "In the other two instances, the kidnappers didn't leave a witness behind. First abduction took place at a dance camp. Shot the teacher in the back before she even saw what was coming. More bullets were lodged in the floor near the ballet bar where the girls stretched. Five girls were taken, ages twelve to fourteen."

Good God. Twelve years old? She was just a baby. Innocent. A girl with no idea what the men had in store for her.

"Second attack was outside a Waco high school. Men snuck up on the cheerleading squad as they were walking to their cars after practice. This time they lay in waiting, snatched them one by one. No casualties. Science teacher was leaving about that time and saw the last of the six girls tossed into the back of a black van. Tinted windows. No tag. Driver raced away just as another girl ran around the corner. She was in the bathroom changing or she would have been taken, too."

"Did she see any of the men well enough to make an ID?"

"Afraid not. She was pretty shook up. Said all she saw was a man's back and the gun he was holding to her friend's head."

"You think we're dealing with the same men or factions of a larger trafficking ring?"

"Hard to say at this point. Unfortunately there weren't any surveillance cameras at the dance camp. There were two in the high-school parking lot, but the assailants shot them out."

Of course they did. "None at the art studio, either," Lucas said. Although he'd advise Ms. Reacher to install a security system if she reopened the studio. "How are the families holding up?"

"About like you'd expect," Tradd said. "They've seen enough TV and news stories to speculate on what's happening. None of it's pretty."

No, it wasn't. Most likely they were being drugged

and held somewhere until they could ship them out of the country or to perspective buyers. They probably had clients waiting.

His stomach knotted. Too many depraved people in the world, and men who'd pay for sex.

The girls who didn't go to a buyer would suffer an equally harsh or worse fate. They'd be put in brothels, forced to work as prostitutes. Treated inhumanely. Beaten. Raped. Sometimes drugged, chained in a room so they couldn't escape.

"Email me the files, crime-scene photos, information on the victims so I can compare." Not that he thought the victims or their families had anything to do with this. This read like a professional hit. The ring targeted random groups that were vulnerable, easily accessible and fit a certain type and age range.

Otherwise, they would have also taken Charlotte Reacher.

Instead, they'd left her for dead.

THE GIRLS WERE SCREAMING. They needed her. She had to help them. Stop the bad men…

Charlotte blinked and tried to open her eyes, but she was so sleepy she couldn't force them open. A few minutes ago, she'd heard someone talking. The nurse, she said her name was Haley. They were moving her to a room.

She'd been shot. Had a head injury. Had undergone surgery.

She was lucky, Haley said. She was alive.

But what about Evie, Adrian and Agnes, and Mae Lynn?

Tears seeped from her aching eyes and trickled down her cheeks.

A warm hand touched hers. Slid over it and squeezed.

She tensed, then realized it felt good. Comforting. And she was cold. So cold inside…she shivered.

"Charlotte, my name is Special Agent Lucas Hawk."

A man's voice. Gruff. Almost tender. Another squeeze of her hand and she realized the hand belonged to the man speaking.

"I know you've been through hell today and you're exhausted, but I need to talk to you. Need to ask you some questions."

She blinked, wanting to see his face, but her eyelids slid closed again. The medication must be weighing her down, drawing her back to the darkness. She wanted to stay there, to be numb and forget, to silence the screams.

"I promise you I won't stay long, but you were shot by some men who came into your art studio. They forced the students in your class to go with them."

Her lungs squeezed for air. She suddenly couldn't breathe. She clawed at the bedding, gasping. A machine beeped. Footsteps clattered, then a woman's stern voice said:

"Sir, you're upsetting her. You have to leave."

"I'm sorry," the man said in a gruff tone. "I won't stay long, but we need her help. The men who shot her kidnapped four teenagers. Time is of the essence. The kidnappers might be moving the girls out of the country as we speak."

The woman mumbled something Charlotte couldn't understand, but the agent's words taunted her.

She had to do what she could to help find her students.

She moaned and reached for his hand. He took it and stroked her palm. The contact gave her hope, and she forced her eyes open.

But the room was dark. Completely dark.

"I need you to tell me anything you remember," Special Agent Lucas Hawk said. "Even the smallest details might help—"

His words became garbled as panic seized Charlotte. She blinked furiously, but a cloudy haze of gray and black shrouded her vision. She couldn't see his face.

Couldn't see anything but an ominous black.

LUCAS STIFFENED. Something was wrong.

Charlotte gasped for a breath, her fingernails digging into his palm. "Help…"

He cradled her hand between both of his, tried to soothe her. "You're safe now, Charlotte. You're in the hospital and you're going to be okay." But those four teenagers weren't.

Dear God, he hated to push her, but they had to act quickly. The men could be halfway across the state by now.

She pushed at the sheets and grabbed the bed rail with her free hand. "I…can't see," she whispered between choked breaths. "I can't see you. I can't see anything."

Lucas's pulse clamored. "You mean you can't see the shooter? You were in the studio, weren't you? Or did you and the girls hide?"

"No… I was there," she cried, her chest heaving. "They stormed in and took them. I tried to save them, but the big one shot me and hit me in the head."

She jerked her hand from his and pressed it to her temple. She winced when she discovered the bandage. Her forehead was bruised and discolored, a knot at her hairline, and she had five stitches.

He leaned over the bed and stroked her arm. "Charlotte, it's okay, I know it was terrifying and you wanted to save your students. Just tell me what you saw and we can still save them."

A sob escaped her, painful and heartbreaking. "I couldn't stop them. I tried to."

"Shh, I know you did. I saw the studio, bullets were everywhere."

She grabbed his arm and pulled him closer, then stared up at him with terror-glazed eyes. "I did try, but I failed and they're gone."

"I'm sorry, that's why I'm here. I need your help, though."

"But I can't see," she cried again. "I can't see anything."

"You mean you didn't get a good look at the men?"

She shook her head wildly. "No, I mean my vision is gone. I can't see you or anything in the room."

A cold chill swept over him. She'd suffered a head injury. The doctor hadn't mentioned anything about her eyes, but it was possible...

"I'll get help." He rushed from the room and spotted the nurse. "Get the doctor. Now."

His commanding tone made the woman's eyes widen, then she raced to the nurses station. A second later, a page sounded over the intercom, then she hurried back toward him. He met her in the doorway.

Her disapproving look speared him. "I told you not to upset her."

"It wasn't me," Lucas said between gritted teeth. "She says she lost her vision."

Alarm flashed on the nurse's face, and she rushed

into the room. Charlotte was lying so still that it sent a bolt of fear through him.

The nurse gently touched Charlotte's arm. "It's Haley, your nurse, Ms. Reacher. The doctor is on his way."

Charlotte turned her head toward the nurse, but the glazed expression in her eyes remained.

Then silent tears began to slide down her cheeks.

THE VAN THE men had put them in bounced over the ruts in the road and threw Evie against the side of the interior.

She bit back a groan of pain, blinked to stem the dizziness then wrestled with the zip ties around her wrists, but they wouldn't budge. Hands bound behind their backs, Adrian and Agnes were curled together in the dark corner. Agnes was sobbing while Adrian talked in low whispers to comfort her. Mae Lynn was lying on her side, her eyes glazed in shock.

When those nasty men had thrown them in the van, Mae Lynn had been screaming. One of them had jammed a gun in her face and threatened to kill her. Mae Lynn had gone quiet and hadn't moved or spoken since.

Terror gripped Evie's chest in a vise, squeezing her lungs. Ms. Charlotte had been shot. Was she dead?

Tears crowded her throat. No… She couldn't be. Ms. Charlotte was the only person in the world who cared about them. She helped Evie see that she might have a future. That bright colors and light existed. That she could paint beautiful pictures and express herself through art.

And that *she* was beautiful even though no family had wanted her as their child.

Agnes's sobs bounced off the dark walls of the van, drawing Evie back to the situation. She had to stay tough. Do something to get them out of here.

But what?

There were four men, and they were all huge. She barely weighed ninety pounds.

And they had guns.

If she could grab one of those guns, she might be able to force them to release her and the others.

She knew how to shoot. That, she'd learned early on.

Everyone thought she was a weakling. But they were wrong.

She'd survived one foster home after another because she studied people. She didn't know what these men wanted with them, but she had an idea.

A shudder coursed through her, and she squashed the thought.

She'd wait for the right moment, then she'd grab one of their guns. No one knew it, but she'd shot a man once. Foster daddy number five.

She'd had to, or be his bitch. That's what he'd called it when he took the other fosters to bed.

She wasn't going to be anybody's bitch. She'd kill whoever tried to make her into one just like she'd shot that bastard, foster five.

Chapter Three

Lucas gritted his teeth as the nurse shoved him from the hospital room into the hallway. A doctor rushed in, and the nurse joined him, leaving Lucas watching through the small window in the door.

The nurse took Charlotte's vitals while the doctor shined a light in Charlotte's eyes. Silent sobs wracked the petite woman's body, her fear palpable.

Was it possible the only witness to this damn trafficking had been blinded in the attack?

"Lucas?"

His brother's voice dragged him from his somber thoughts.

"What happened? Is she all right?"

"I don't know." Lucas exhaled sharply. "She just woke up from surgery."

"Have you talked to her?"

"I was trying to, but she got upset and the nurse made me leave."

"She's in shock," Harrison said.

Lucas's stomach knotted as the doctor tried to calm Charlotte. The nurse injected something into her IV. Probably a sedative.

Lucas folded his arms. "The head injury may have caused her to lose her vision."

Harrison cursed. "What did the doctor say?"

"He's examining her now," Lucas said. "Before then she was pretty groggy. She didn't say much except that she tried to save the girls, but the men opened fire."

Damn, he didn't like the picture that painted.

"I asked my deputy to notify the foster parents in person and to see if they'd noticed anyone suspicious hanging around their houses. Someone stalking the girls."

"Good idea," Lucas said. "Also, ask him if one of the foster parents seemed suspicious. We had a case once where a stepfather actually sold a girl for money to buy drugs."

"Good God," Harrison said. "What did the mother say when she found out?"

Lucas grimaced. "Hell, she was too strung out to even notice the girl was gone." Lucas and his brothers were damn lucky to have had the family they'd grown up in. In spite of their troubles and trauma over losing Chrissy, his mother had hung in there. If only his father had...

"Find out if any of the girls had computers at their foster homes. If so, confiscate them and send them to the lab. It's possible our kidnappers contacted the girls online. There, they can find out personal information about them, who their friends are, if they belong to a club or group, what their schedules are..."

"So they may be cyberstalking their victims, looking for groups to target?" Harrison said.

Lucas nodded. "Social media has opened up a new

hunting ground for predators. People pretending to be someone they aren't. Scam artists. Pedophiles."

"I'll get right on it."

The doctor walked to the door, his expression concerned.

"How is she, Doctor?" Lucas asked.

The older man narrowed his eyes. "Are you family?"

"No." Lucas flashed his FBI credentials and Harrison indicated his sheriff's badge. "We're investigating the shooting that put Ms. Reacher in here," Lucas said.

Harrison cleared his throat. "We're also trying to find the four girls abducted from Ms. Reacher's studio. If she saw something, it's imperative we speak to her ASAP."

The doctor ran a hand through his thick gray hair. "I understand the situation, but under the circumstances, my patient needs rest. We have to run tests to determine the extent of her injuries. I'm calling in a specialist, ordering a CAT scan, MRI and full neurological."

Lucas glanced through the window and saw Charlotte roll over in the bed to face the door. Compassion for her filled him. She'd obviously been traumatized and needed time to heal.

But every minute that passed meant the trafficking ring could be getting farther and farther away from Tumbleweed. And that any chance of rescuing Charlotte's students would be lost.

CHARLOTTE FOUGHT DESPAIR as she lay in the dark. She needed to do something to help find her students, but she was so groggy from the medication they'd pumped through her that she could barely function.

The doctor said her blindness could be temporary.

Which meant it could also be permanent.

No, she had to hold out hope that she would see again. Even if she didn't, she had to pull herself together and talk to that FBI agent. He wanted to find Evie and Mae Lynn and Agnes and Adrian.

She needed his help to do it more than she'd ever needed anyone in her life.

She hated being needy.

But the girls' lives depended on her swallowing her pride, not wallowing in self-pity and fear.

Still, she was so tired she drifted to sleep. Sometime later, she woke up and realized she was in the midst of an MRI. She drifted in and out of consciousness through that procedure and the CAT scan, but couldn't keep her eyes open as they wheeled her down the hall.

The nightmares of the day plagued her. The bullets pinging off the floor and wall around her. The girls' terrified screams...

That group was the closest thing to family she'd had in a long time.

She had to fight her way back so she could find them. If she didn't, she'd never forgive herself.

WHILE LUCAS AND Harrison waited on Charlotte to undergo tests, Lucas brought Harrison up-to-date on the abductions in Abilene and Waco.

"Sounds like the same group," Harrison said. "Were the other victims foster kids?"

"No," Lucas said. "One case involved dance students at a ballet camp, the other, cheerleaders from a high school. The ballet instructor was shot and died instantly. No witnesses. Girls at the ballet camp were from various parts of Texas."

"So these guys aren't targeting a specific type, just females between the ages of twelve and eighteen."

Lucas nodded.

"Sick," Harrison muttered.

"Definitely," Lucas agreed. "Human trafficking is a widespread problem and has touched every major city in the US." Although Tumbleweed was just a small town...

Harrison spread pictures of the missing girls on the table in the waiting room. "These photographs correspond with the names of the girls in the class scheduled at that time, but we should confirm with Charlotte that they were in fact the ones abducted."

Lucas's heart hammered as he studied the pictures. All young and vulnerable, mere teens.

Prime targets for predators.

Lucas noticed the nurse slip Charlotte back into her room. He walked over and peered through the window again. Charlotte was agitated, waving her hands.

The nurse rushed to the door, and Lucas braced himself for her to tell him to leave her alone. Instead, she motioned for him to come in.

"She wants to see you. I told her she should rest, but she insists it's important."

Lucas's pulse jumped. Maybe she had a clue to help them find these bastards.

CHARLOTTE WAS SO exhausted that all she wanted to do was fade back into sleep and forget the horror that had happened today. Forget that four of her students were missing, and that she was blind.

The doctor said she needed time for the swelling to go down. The possibility she might need surgery existed, but they wouldn't discuss that yet.

Footsteps sounded and the door to her room squeaked shut. Her lungs tightened.

"Haley? Doctor?"

"No, Charlotte, it's me. Agent Lucas Hawk, Harrison's brother." The footsteps again, soft, as if he was controlling the sound, working to be quiet. "But you can call me Lucas."

Call him Lucas? She didn't even know him. Although she'd seen pictures of all the Hawk men, and Lucas was the most virile, handsome one of the bunch. He was also the most intimidating.

But his gruff voice was soothing, caring…almost sensual.

She thumbed her hand through her hair, self-conscious when what her fingers connected with was sticky, matted. Blood from her head wound must have soaked the strands. She probably looked a mess.

Not that she should care. But she had the sudden urge to see herself in a mirror, to know just how deep the injury was. To know if she'd have a bad scar.

A dark chuckle bubbled in her chest as she realized she might never be able to look in a mirror again.

Footsteps again, then the scent of the agent's masculine aftershave wafted toward her. A musky odor that was pleasant, sensual, like his voice.

"You told the nurse that you wanted to see me? That it was important." He paused. "What is it, Charlotte?"

"I'm sorry about earlier," she whispered.

His hand gently brushed her shoulder. "You have nothing to be sorry about. You've been through a terrible ordeal today. I hate to bother you, but the longer we wait, the more time it gives these bastards to escape."

"I know," Charlotte said, battling tears. "They could be out of the country. We can't let that happen."

"No, we can't," Lucas said. "Can you tell me the names of the girls they abducted?"

Charlotte twisted the sheets in her hands. "Evie, she's thirteen. Mae Lynn is fifteen. Agnes and Adrian are sisters. Agnes is sixteen and Adrian fourteen." Her voice cracked with emotion.

"All right," he said quietly. "Just take your time and describe what happened. What you saw and heard."

Charlotte sniffed. "We were in the middle of class. I should have had the door locked." Guilt sucker punched her. "But it was midafternoon so I thought we were safe."

"Don't beat yourself up. This was not your fault. Tumbleweed is a small town. Most businesses don't lock their doors during work hours," Lucas said.

Charlotte latched on to his words. "But if I had—"

"Stop," the agent said more firmly. "Again, it wasn't your fault. Playing the what-if game won't help. Let's just focus on what the men looked like, anything they said. There were four of them?"

She stiffened. "How did you know that?"

"Because we believe they're the same group who struck in Abilene and Waco. Could be different hired men, but connected."

The implications he suggested sank in. "It's an organized group?"

"Yes, they're professionals," Lucas said. "Four armed and masked men strike, and kidnap teenage girls. So far they haven't left any witnesses behind."

A chill of foreboding washed over Charlotte. She was lucky to have survived.

They'd probably thought she was dead.

"Can you describe any of the men?"

Charlotte swallowed back bile. The pain was making her nauseous.

He continued in a gruff voice. "Were they tall? Short? Big? Small?"

She struggled to see the men in her mind's eye. "One was a big guy, tall, heavy, he seemed to be the leader. It happened so fast—we were painting, then the men rushed in. The leader ordered us not to move, then I realized they all had guns. I offered them money—"

"They didn't want money," Lucas said bluntly.

She shook her head. "The big one slammed his gun against my head. I fell and was dizzy, then the others started snatching the girls. They're young, but they've been through hell and they're tough." Maybe that toughness would help them survive. "They screamed and fought, and tried to escape. I tried to stop them but..." Her voice trailed off, her throat clogging with tears.

"But they shot you," Lucas said.

She nodded, swiping angrily at the tears that fell. "Then the leader hit me in the head again, and the others dragged the girls out the door. I crawled after them, but I was too late."

THE IMAGE OF Charlotte's bloody handprints on the floor taunted Lucas. She was a petite woman, but she'd made it to the door. Anger shot through him. He wanted to hurt these guys bad.

"You said you crawled to the door," Lucas said. "Did you see what kind of vehicle they were driving?"

Charlotte inhaled a deep breath as if struggling to piece her memory together.

"Was it a car? An SUV? A van?"

"A van," she whispered. "Black. Tinted windows."

Lucas's pulse jumped. The teacher in Waco had also mentioned a black van. "A minivan or full-size?"

"Cargo," Charlotte said in a pained voice.

"That's good, Charlotte. How about a license plate?"

Her brows furrowed together, the bandage on her forehead stark against her ivory skin. "I didn't see a tag."

"Was there any writing or a logo on the side?"

"I don't think so." Her face crumpled. "It happened so fast…"

"You did good, Charlotte." Hopefully she'd remember more as time passed. "Think about the men now. Did any of them have any distinguishing marks? A mustache or goatee? Scar? Tattoo?"

This time she pressed both hands over her face and rubbed her eyes. "The big one, the leader, had a tattoo on his hand. A snake." She paused. "His face was covered with a mask, but I think there was some kind of tattoo on his neck, too. It looked like a bolt of lightning."

"Good work, Charlotte. These details could be helpful."

He quickly texted the analyst at the Bureau the information. Keenan Hart was thirty, smart, and obsessive about details.

She quickly responded with a return text.

Black van reported in the Waco kidnapping. Authorities already on the look for it. Researching tattoos now.

When he looked up, Charlotte's eyes were closing. Sensing she was about to fade again, he hurried to ask his last question. "One more thing, Charlotte."

She moaned softly. "Hmm?"

"Did all of the men speak English or did one of them speak another language?"

She twisted her head toward him as if she could see him, but the blankness glazed her eyes again. "The leader was really the only one who talked. He spoke English."

"Did he have an accent?"

She frowned. "I don't think so. Why? Do you think they're foreign?"

His gut tightened. He'd suspected Columbian or Eastern European. But without witnesses to the other kidnappings, that was a guess.

His phone beeped with a text. Harrison.

Black cargo van spotted outside Tumbleweed at an abandoned warehouse. Meet me downstairs and we'll check it out.

Hope made Lucas's adrenaline spike, and he placed his hand over Charlotte's. Her hand was small and delicate, and her skin felt soft, feminine.

Thankfully, she was tougher than she looked.

"Charlotte, I may have a lead on that van. Harrison and I are going to check it out. Get some rest."

She nodded weakly although she was already drifting asleep.

He smiled at her, then sadly realized that even if she was awake, she couldn't see him. The thought bothered him more than he wanted to admit.

All the more reason he'd track down these sons of bitches and put them away.

Determination kicking in, he hurried to the elevator, rode to the lobby and rushed outside to meet his brother.

Harrison was talking to Honey on the phone. When he hung up, emotions clouded his face. "I broke the news to Honey. She's going to pick up some flowers, then visit Charlotte in a little while."

They hurried to his brother's SUV, and Harrison sped from the hospital parking lot. "Any more word on Charlotte's condition?"

"No. She's trying to be strong, but she's hurting and scared." Lucas tensed. "Doc says the blindness might be temporary. They have to wait on the swelling to go down. That might take a while. Days. Maybe weeks."

Harrison's expression turned grim, and they fell into silence as his brother maneuvered through town then veered onto the road leading to Dead Man's Bluff.

This place held bad memories for them both.

"Those warehouses have been abandoned for so long I'd forgotten about them," Harrison said.

Lucas nodded agreement.

But they would be the perfect place to hold the girls until they could move them to the buyers.

CHARLOTTE'S SHOULDER THROBBED, the pain intensifying as images of the kidnappers flashed through her mind. They had stolen the girls she was in charge of, girls she loved. Girls she was supposed to help.

The door squeaked. Her eyes flew open, but the black nothingness filled her vision.

Then a footstep. And another. So soft that she had to lie perfectly still to hear it.

"Lucas?"

A hushed sound. Breathing. Deep breathing. But no voice.

Terror seized her. "Agent Hawk? Harrison?"

No answer.

She reached for the call button, fumbling along the bed to find it.

The acrid odor of cigarettes wafted toward her.

Dear God, the leader of the kidnappers had smelled like cigarettes.

Had he come back to kill her?

Chapter Four

Cold fear pressed against Charlotte's chest. Lucas said that the men who'd taken her students had struck before and had never left a witness behind.

Had one of them come here to finish the job he'd begun?

She was stone-still and held her breath, hoping whoever was in the room would think she was unconscious and leave. If not for the scent of cigarette smoke and the fact that he hadn't said anything, she might think it was a doctor.

But doctors identified themselves.

Footsteps padded softly. Every cell in her body tensed with anticipation. Her left arm was hooked to an IV. All he had to do was inject her with a drug that would seep into her system and she'd drift into oblivion. No one would ever be the wiser.

She did not want to die.

Another footstep. The tray table made a noise as he pushed it away from her.

His breath punctuated the silence. The bed jarred as he bumped it.

She finally found the call button and pressed it, praying the nurse or a staff member would come quickly.

Her lungs ached for air. She slowly released her breath, straining not to make a sound or rustle the covers.

"Ms. Reacher," a deep voice murmured. "Are you awake?"

She lay perfectly still, careful not to flinch or even bat an eye.

"I hate to disturb you, but my name is Gerald Ingram, I'm with the police. I need to ask you some questions about what happened at your art studio."

He was a cop?

She slowly released a breath. But questions nagged at her. If he was investigating, why hadn't he been with Harrison or Lucas?

In spite of her efforts at control, her breath wheezed out, shaky and rattling in the tense silence.

Being in the dark heightened her other senses. If she could see his face, she might be able to tell if he was lying or out to hurt her.

"Ms. Reacher, I know you were injured and underwent surgery, but the men who shot you kidnapped four of your students. Can you describe them?"

Tears burned the backs of her eyelids, desperate to escape. In her mind, she pictured Adrian and Agnes, and Mae Lynn and sweet Evie. What was happening to them?

If the men planned to sell them as sex slaves, hopefully they wouldn't hurt them, at least not physically. That would mess up their product.

But the girls must be terrified.

Another nudge from the man's hand. "Ma'am, I need a statement about what happened. Did any of the men call each other by name?"

She searched her memory. Had one of them spoken a name?

"You're the only one who can help," the man said again. "Please talk to me. You do want to help find those girls before something bad happens to them, don't you?"

Anger shot through her, and she opened her eyes. Darkness. Not even a sliver of light.

"So you are awake?" he said with a hint of sarcasm to his tone. "Now, what—"

"Excuse me." A woman's voice echoed from across the room, and Charlotte realized the door had opened. The nurse. Finally.

"Sir, you aren't supposed to be in here," Haley said.

"If Ms. Reacher can identify the men who kidnapped her students, she needs to speak up."

Rustling of clothes and footsteps sounded as Haley approached. "Ms. Reacher has cooperated with the sheriff and FBI already. She's just undergone surgery and needs her rest."

The man's hand brushed hers. "Come on, Charlotte," he said impatiently, "give me something."

She blinked rapidly, her head throbbing with confusion, and the memory of the gunshots and girls' cries.

A machine beeped. Her heart monitor? Blood pressure?

This time a softer hand. Haley. "It's all right, Charlotte, it's all right."

"What's wrong with her?" the man snapped. "She's going to make it, isn't she?"

"Yes, but you need to leave."

"But she hasn't told me anything," he protested.

"And she's not going to," Haley said. "Now, either leave or I'll call security."

The man protested again.

"Now," Haley ordered.

Emotion bubbled to the surface, threatening to spill over. Charlotte hated being in the dark, and at the mercy of others.

Footsteps again, then the door closed. Her chest heaved as she breathed out.

Then Haley was back. "I'm sorry about that."

"He said he was a cop," Charlotte said.

"He was no cop," Haley said with a grunt of disgust. "That man is a reporter, and not a nice one. He'll do anything for a story."

Charlotte closed her eyes, grateful she hadn't said anything to him. She'd instantly felt uneasy with him.

Not like she had with Lucas. He'd made her feel safe.

The reporter's name replayed in her head. She vaguely recalled seeing him on the news. Haley was right.

He was ruthless. Had been known to run with a story without verifying the facts or his source. Had interviewed victims of crimes before and implied they were at fault for being victimized.

What kind of garbage would he air about her?

LUCAS SCANNED THE area as he and Harrison approached the abandoned warehouses. They were only a few miles from the cave at Dead Man's Bluff where they'd found his sister's body.

The gruesome image of her bones lying beside two other young girls' skeletons would haunt him forever. The fact that she'd lain there dead for almost two decades made matters worse. All that time they'd searched for her, and struggled to hold on to hope that somehow she was alive.

But her disappearance turned out to be a tragic accident. A mentally challenged boy named Elden had wanted to make friends with Chrissy, but he hadn't realized his strength, and he'd smothered her to death. His mother had protected him. Unfortunately, Chrissy wasn't his only victim.

Harrison's police SUV bounced over the rugged terrain, gravel and dirt spewing.

A row of three warehouses popped into view as Harrison steered the vehicle over a small hill. A rusted-out black cargo van sat by the building.

Except this van had been burned and only the charred shell remained.

Lucas's pulse jumped. If the trafficking ring had brought the girls here to house them until they moved them to buyers, they might have left the girls inside.

The area looked desolate, the warehouses weathered, the steel siding dingy. The Texas sun faded to night, casting shadows across the rugged land.

"It looks deserted," Harrison said.

"We need to check inside the spaces," Lucas said. "You'd be shocked at some places traffickers hold women and children. Boats, storage containers, old barns, the back of cargo vans and trucks. Damn inhumane."

Harrison's mouth tightened as he closed the distance to the warehouses. "Hard to imagine people buying and selling children and women like they're cattle."

Except they might treat cattle with more care. Although if selling the girls at auction to the highest bidder was their game, they would try to preserve the girls' physical appearance.

No visible bruising or injuries.

They'd probably use drugs to keep them under control.

Gears ground, brakes squeaking as Harrison slowed the SUV and swung to a stop. Lucas eased his car door open and slid from the seat, senses honed as he scanned the area between the warehouses.

He and Harrison both pulled their guns, and he braced for trouble as they walked past the charred van then toward the warehouses. Harrison shined a pocket flashlight across the ground.

Lucas did the same, then motioned to Harrison that he spotted tire tracks. He veered right to check the warehouse on the end, while Harrison went left. Gravel crunched beneath his boots as he approached, and he paused to listen at the doorway. He expected it to be locked, but the bolt that had held it closed had been cut and sat in a pile of weeds to the side.

He leaned against the door edge and listened, hoping to hear the sound of girls' voices, something to indicate they were inside.

But he heard nothing.

Frustration knotted his stomach as he eased the door open and aimed the light inside. The space was empty.

Dammit.

Still, he inched inside to search in case there was a room, a box, or a cage hidden in the darkened space.

CHARLOTTE FADED INTO a restless sleep and dreamed that a reporter was in the room snapping photographs of her. She woke, her pulse hammering.

Inhaling to calm her raging heart, she listened for signs the man had returned.

As a child, she'd been self-conscious of her port-wine birthmark. That image of her remained locked in her head, and reminded her that she had once been debilitated by it. No one had wanted her as their child. People had stared and made cruel remarks. Other children had been afraid that if they touched her, that stain would rub off on them.

Tears pricked at her eyes. She blinked furiously to stem them, searching for some semblance of light in the room, but blackness prevailed. Still, she ran her fingers over her cheek, remembering the pain of looking different and wondering if her face or eyes were scarred or appeared unusual.

If the morning paper or news would show her lying in bed, weak and vulnerable, the details of her sordid childhood exposed for the world to see.

Guilt and shame quickly overrode her concern—how could she possibly worry about her looks or people reading about her past when her students needed her? No telling what they were going through.

Her breathing turned erratic again, and she suddenly felt like her chest was going to explode. Pain shot through her, stifling and frightening. One of the monitors went off, the beeping more rapid with the tune of her breathing.

The door screeched open, then footsteps. "Ms. Reacher, I'm here." Haley's voice, soothing and calm. Her hand gently brushed Charlotte's. "Did something happen?"

Charlotte shook her head. "A nightmare."

"That's understandable. You've been through hell," the nurse said.

Charlotte gasped for a breath again, that tight sensation returning.

"Just try to relax, take slow even breaths."

"What's happening?" Charlotte asked, her voice cracking as she clawed for air.

"You're having a panic attack," Haley said softly. "It's not uncommon, especially after suffering a trauma. Try to imagine yourself in a happy place."

Charlotte nodded miserably and forced herself to do as Haley instructed. Slow breaths. Think of a happy place.

Her studio. The paints. The vibrant colors. Reds and blues and purples, shades of violet. Yellow, like the sunflowers she adored. Then pastels. The pale yellow of the moon on a cool night when she gazed at the stars. The light blue of the sky on a sunny day, of the ocean at sunset.

Except the attack had tainted the image of the studio. Her happy place was no longer tranquil or peaceful, but shrouded in the horror of what had happened.

No, she couldn't let those men destroy her place, or the good that had happened in the studio.

The girls were painting, laughing, talking, listening to music. Their hearts were opening as they poured emotions onto the canvases, their spirits lifting as they began to trust her and each other.

"It's going to be all right," Haley said.

How could it be when she might never see her students again?

LUCAS SCANNED THE interior of the warehouse space, but it appeared to be empty. Knowing that appearances could be deceiving, he crept inside, senses alert in case the girls had been locked inside a cage or an underground space.

It had happened before. A woman buried in a box beneath the ground. They hadn't found her in time.

He prayed it was different for these young girls.

The flashlight painted a thin stream across the cement flooring, and he inched through the space, crossing to the back. Several barrels were pushed against the wall.

His heart raced as he rapped his knuckles on the exterior. A hollow sound echoed back. Still, he pried open the tops and searched each one.

Empty.

He didn't know whether to be relieved or disappointed.

Satisfied the space was clean, he crept through the back door and outside, then searched the bushes and grounds until he reached the middle warehouse.

Just as made it to the door, a screeching sound came from the interior.

Pulse jumping, he braced his gun and slipped through the opening. It was pitch-dark inside. The noise...there it was again.

A high-pitched wail.

Holding his breath, he aimed his flashlight along the wall, searching for the source. A wooden crate was pushed to the back.

Dear God. Was someone inside?

Chapter Five

The wailing sounded again.

Lucas rushed to the crate, anxious to see if someone was trapped inside. He examined the wood, noting spaces between the slits. It was about a twelve-by-twelve space.

He needed to open the damn thing. He used his hands to pry at the rotting boards. They easily gave way and he yanked off three of them to look inside.

Nothing.

Damn. Where had that sound come from?

He turned and shined his flashlight across the back wall. A pile of rubbish, old cans, wood, storage containers and trash. Determined to find the source of the wailing, he tossed aside all the junk.

Something moved behind the rubbish. Too small to be a person. An animal?

Sweat beaded on his forehead as he stooped down and dug away more debris. A small orange ball caught his eye. Then a low whine, like a baby crying.

A kitten.

Breath whooshing out in relief, he gently reached inside the space and scooped up the tiny feline.

Growing up on the ranch, he and his brothers had taken in stray dogs, but Chrissy had been the cat lover.

Pain squeezed at his chest. She would have loved this little bundle of fur.

He nuzzled it next to his cheek. "Come on, little one, we'll find you a home."

Satisfied this warehouse hadn't been used for the kidnapped girls, he carried the kitten outside. Harrison was standing by the last warehouse looking grim.

Lucas's heart lurched. "What?"

"It's empty, but it has been used." Harrison narrowed his eyes at the kitten, but didn't comment, then motioned for Lucas to follow him inside the other space.

The interior was dark, but Harrison illuminated a path with his flashlight, and Lucas followed. In the far right corner, he spotted three old mattresses, discarded paper products from take-out restaurants and several empty water bottles.

But it was the hooks on the wall that made his blood run cold. Metal hooks connected to chains.

A used hypodermic lay discarded on the floor, a sign the kidnappers had drugged their victims.

"There's blood on the chains," Harrison said as he pointed to a dark stain.

Nausea climbed Lucas's throat, anger churning at the images that flashed across his mind.

"Let's collect some of this stuff and send it to the lab. Maybe we can confirm who was here and the kidnappers' drug of choice."

Harrison nodded, yanked on gloves and picked up one of the used fast-food bags. "Food looks crusted and moldy inside."

"They didn't bring Charlotte's students here," Lucas said.

"But there were others," Harrison said.

Lucas gritted his teeth. "Which means this trafficking ring may have been scoping out Tumbleweed a lot longer than we think."

Harrison scowled. "Do you think it's possible that someone in town is part of the operation?"

Good question.

Although none of them wanted to believe that their home town was hiding a ring of child traffickers, they couldn't discount the possibility.

CHARLOTTE WAS DREAMING about the girls again—they were screaming. Then one of the men grabbed her and dragged her toward the door with them.

She jerked awake, her breath choking out. She was still in the hospital. Dear God, she wished they'd taken her, too. At least she could have watched over the girls.

"Charlotte?"

Her fingers dug into the bedding as the sound of the hospital door closing echoed in the cold room. Then footsteps. Soft this time.

The voice had been a woman. Not the nurse, though.

A gentle hand covered hers. "Charlotte, it's me, Honey."

Relief surged through her, and she reached for Honey's hand. She'd met Honey when she was searching for a house, and they'd instantly connected and become friends. She liked Honey's knack for taking crumbling properties and houses and turning them into welcoming, beautiful, loving homes. "I'm glad you're here."

Honey pulled her hand into hers. "I'm so sorry about what happened, Charlotte. How do you feel?"

Honey's concern touched her deeply. Charlotte had

been in and out of so many foster homes that she'd never gotten close to anyone.

One family had a scruffy rescue dog that she'd loved. Leaving it had ripped out her heart. Since then, she hadn't allowed herself a pet, either.

"Charlotte, sweetie, talk to me," Honey said softly.

Emotion clogged her throat. Honey was the closest thing Charlotte had ever had to a sister. "I'm terrified for those girls. They should be laughing and shopping for outfits for school dances, not being terrorized by monsters who want to turn them into sex slaves."

Honey pressed a kiss to Charlotte's hand. "I know, it's horrible."

"I keep dreaming about the girls screaming for help. I can hear them crying, but I can't do anything." Her voice cracked. "I hate being helpless."

"Harrison and Lucas are doing everything possible to find them." Honey stroked Charlotte's hand to calm her. "They won't stop until they bring them back and put those horrid men in prison."

"But they could be on a boat or plane out of the country," Charlotte said. "You hear about cases where young women are kidnapped and never seen again." Evie's face haunted her, followed by Adrian's and Agnes's and Mae Lynn's. "The girls in my group have already been through hell. But this—this could be more than they can bear." Especially fragile Mae Lynn. She'd been a cutter before she'd joined the group.

Honey's quiet breathing whispered in the air. "Listen to me, Charlotte. I know those girls have had it rough, but they're like you and me, they're tough. Survivors. Harrison and Lucas will find them, then they're going to need you." She paused. "So the best thing you can do for them is to focus on your own recovery."

Charlotte blinked back tears. "But all I can think about is Evie and Mae Lynn—"

"Shh," Honey whispered. "You don't know the Hawk brothers like I do. They're the most trustworthy, brave, courageous, strong men I know. When they say they're going to do something, they'll do it."

Charlotte wanted to believe her. But she'd never trusted a man in her life.

Honey released her hand and disappeared for a moment. When she returned she dragged a chair up beside the bed, and dabbed at Charlotte's tearstained face with a tissue.

"Does your head hurt?"

Charlotte licked her dry lips. "Yes, but it doesn't matter—"

"It does matter," Honey said with conviction. "You matter to me, Charlotte." Honey's voice cracked. "I know it must be scary to open your eyes and not be able to see."

"I always hated the dark," Charlotte admitted.

"Me, too," Honey said softly.

Charlotte squeezed Honey's hand and blinked back tears. Maybe her friend was right. She had to be strong. Dig deep. Heal herself.

She wouldn't be any good to the girls if she fell apart.

LUCAS CALLED A crime-scene investigative team to search the warehouses and surrounding area, and to process the interior of the building, where they'd found the chains and blood. He and Harrison had done all they could do, but didn't want to miss anything. Even a partial print or button from one of the kidnappers could help.

His phone buzzed, and he settled the kitten in the SUV. He didn't know what he was going to do with it, but he didn't intend to leave it out here to fend for itself.

Maybe his mother would want it. Or Honey. Or... Charlotte.

Hell, what was he thinking? He didn't even know the woman. She might not like cats. And no telling how long she'd be hospitalized.

"Lucas, it's Tradd."

The agent's voice jerked him back to the present. "What's up?"

"Did you find anything?" Tradd asked.

"We're at some warehouses outside Tumbleweed that appear to have been a holding place for victims, although judging from discarded food containers, they've been gone a while. We don't think it's the Tumbleweed victims."

"These crews know how to slide in and out under the radar," Tradd said.

"What about you guys?" Lucas asked.

"I'm on my way to the Mexican border," Tradd said. "Got a tip from a CI to check out. Agent Sandino is en route to Miami to look at some containers we suspect the traffickers might be using to transport the human cargo."

Human cargo. Those two words shouldn't be used in the same sentence.

"I'll keep you posted." Tradd ended the call and Lucas hurried to meet Harrison by his SUV. The crime team had arrived and they were combing the warehouse space, processing the charred van and searching the property. If there had been trouble with one or more of the girls or one had escaped, they might find someone in those woods.

The next three hours were grueling as they combed the area. Lucas and Harrison joined in, searching behind trees, rocks, in the ditches and a section of ground that looked as if it had been disturbed.

The dirt was piled high with leaves and brush spread across it. A grave?

Lucas jammed a shovel into the dirt, and proceeded to clear away the soil, leaves and sticks, while Harrison explored another section that had been covered up as if it led to a tunnel or a cave.

Lucas held his breath as he dug deeper and deeper. The shovel hit something hard, and a sick knot clenched in his stomach.

Was it bones? Or a body?

Chapter Six

Praying it wasn't one of Charlotte's students, Lucas dropped to his knees and dug with his hands, tossing aside dirt and leaves. Harrison yanked sticks, leaves and branches away from the space behind him that appeared to be a hidden cave.

Voices echoed from the woods. A coyote howled in the distance.

Dammit, he dug faster. His fingers hit something hard. He felt the surface. Jagged. A large stone.

Not a body.

Thank God.

For a moment, he was so relieved that he leaned his head on his arm and simply focused on breathing.

"Lucas?"

Harrison's voice made him jerk his head around. The grimness in his brother's eyes twisted Lucas's stomach.

"Did you find something?"

"I'm afraid so," Harrison said.

Lucas stood, dread rolling through him. Just a short time ago, he and his brothers had searched a cave not too far from here and found his sister's remains.

"One of our girls from Tumbleweed?" Lucas asked.

Harrison shook his head. "I don't think so. This body has been there too long."

Lucas stiffened. "You think it could have been one of Elden's victims that we don't know about?"

Harrison shrugged. "I doubt it. His mother came clean after we made the arrest. Once we identify her, we can find out if she was a kidnap victim, a runaway or…a victim of another crime."

Harrison phoned the ME while Lucas crossed to the cave entrance and ducked through the opening.

Sure enough, a skeleton was inside, brittle hair rotting along with the corpse.

Lucas shined the light around the bones, searching for any way to identify the girl, but there was no ID or wallet. Her clothes were decaying on her bones, yet he could see that three of her fingers looked broken.

Defense wounds?

Or she'd broken them trying to claw her way out of her chains in that damn warehouse. An image of her escaping taunted him, followed by another image of her being chased in the woods.

Harrison poked his head in. "The ME and CSI are on their way."

Lucas nodded and exited the cave, his anger blending with grief over the dead girl.

He hadn't known her but her young life had been snuffed out way too soon.

CHARLOTTE'S EYES FELT heavy again. "Thank you for coming, Honey," Charlotte said. "I have no idea what time it is, but if you need to go home, please go. I'll be fine."

"I'm not leaving until I hear from the guys." She

patted Charlotte's hand again. "But you need to rest, so sleep, Charlotte. I'll wake you when I hear from them."

The need to close her eyes tugged at Charlotte, although even when she did, the darkness grew blacker. She couldn't erase the images of what had happened earlier or the sounds of her students' cries. "Why did they target me and my students?" she asked, thinking out loud.

"I don't know," Honey said. "Harrison said that they're part of a larger group so it was probably random. They probably scope out local businesses or areas where they can find female groups." She brushed Charlotte's hair away from her forehead again. "But this wasn't your fault. No one could have known what they were planning or where they were going to hit. And you certainly couldn't have stopped them."

Funny how Honey could read her mind. When she'd heard Honey's story of growing up in Tumbleweed, Charlotte had instantly been drawn to her. Honey reminded her of herself.

She was a survivor.

Sweet Evie's face flashed in her mind, along with her other students. Those girls were survivors, too.

The throbbing in her head intensified, and she lifted her hand and touched the bandage. The movement caused her shoulder to ache where she'd been shot.

"Do you need more pain meds?" Honey asked.

An image of herself as a child with that port-wine birthmark returned to haunt her. She wasn't a little kid anymore, but she knew her forehead had taken a bashing. "No, I'm okay." She refused to complain and wanted to clear her head. "Can I ask you something, Honey?"

Honey stroked her arm. "Of course, Charlotte. What is it?"

She felt silly for asking, but she had to face the truth. "Is my face, my eyes, am I…going to be scarred?"

Honey sighed softly. "According to your doctor, you have a half-dozen stitches, but they're in your hairline, and the wound should heal." She paused. "I know you've lost your vision for now, but your eyes look normal, Charlotte."

Charlotte blinked back more tears. "That sounded vain, and it's really not important, especially considering my students are in danger—"

"It doesn't sound vain," Honey assured her. "It's only human to wonder. Besides, you and I are alike, Charlotte. We both have to know what we're dealing with, then we face it head-on."

Charlotte's throat closed. Honey was right.

When she'd first heard how awful some of the locals had treated her friend, she wasn't sure she wanted to settle in Tumbleweed. But Honey's giving spirit had made her want to call this place home.

Only now, her studio had been trashed, her future ripped apart and the kids she devoted her heart and time to help were missing.

LUCAS'S PHONE BUZZED as Harrison drove away from the ranch. Thankfully, his mother had been thrilled to have the kitten. He'd known she was lonely and should have thought of getting her a pet sooner.

Harrison veered onto the road leading to the hospital. Lucas connected the call. Keenan Hart from the Bureau.

"I've been researching those tattoos," Keenan said.

"Snakes are common, and I've found several lightning bolts. I need more details. It would help if Charlotte would look at photos—"

"I'm afraid that's not possible," Lucas said grimly. "She lost her sight. The doctor doesn't know if it's temporary or permanent."

"Oh, gosh, I'm sorry. I'll send you the photos of the ones I found and you can describe them to her."

"Good idea." Lucas explained about the body they'd discovered at the warehouse and the charred van. "Also, run background checks on the victims' foster families. Check their financials for trouble."

"You think one of them is involved?" Keenan asked.

"I'm just covering the bases," Lucas said. If a foster parent had been bribed or paid off, he could use that as leverage to push him—or her—for more information about the kidnappers.

Before he hung up, his phone buzzed again.

"Keep me posted," he told Keenan, and then clicked to answer. "Brayden?"

"Yeah, I'm here with Mom. She was upset about what happened in town today."

Everybody in town was probably upset. Missing children had a way of inciting panic and fear.

"Reassure her that we're doing everything we can to find the missing teens," Lucas said.

"I have, but that's not the reason I called. We were watching TV, Lucas, and the story is plastered all over the place. It made national news."

Lucas scrubbed a hand through his hair. Of course it had.

"Some reporter named Gerald Ingram showed a picture of Charlotte in the hospital."

"What the hell?"

"He announced that she was the only surviving witness."

A litany of curse words spewed from Lucas's tongue. "That idiot bastard. He might as well have put a bullet in her head."

"I know. I'm sorry, man. Is there anything I can do?"

"Just stay with Mom for a while."

They said goodbye just as Harrison pulled into the hospital parking lot.

"What happened?" his brother asked as they parked and walked toward the entrance.

Lucas relayed the news about the reporter. "I should have posted security at Charlotte's door," Harrison said.

"I should have thought of it, too." But they'd both been too anxious to track down that van and look for the kidnapped victims. "I'll stay with her tonight," Lucas offered. "Tomorrow we'll assign a detail."

Harrison nodded, and they went inside and rode the elevator to the second floor. With that damn news report on his mind, Lucas scanned the halls and corridors in case one of the kidnappers returned to try and take out Charlotte.

CHARLOTTE WAS ROUSED from sleep again as footsteps echoed in the room. Then voices.

"How's she doing, Honey?"

Harrison. She heard the smack of his lips as he kissed Honey, stirring other emotions inside her. She'd watched those lovebirds with envy the last couple of months.

Harrison was lucky to have found a wonderful woman

like Honey. She was lucky, too. Harrison seemed completely devoted to his wife.

"She's been resting some," Honey said.

"That reporter Gerald Ingram just aired the story that Charlotte survived."

This time, Lucas. His voice was slightly deeper than Harrison's. And darker. Intimidating.

"Oh, my God," Honey said. "That's not good, is it?"

"Afraid not," Harrison said grimly.

Charlotte shifted, pushing herself higher on the pillow to prop up. The room blurred into darkness, but she sensed the presence of Honey and Harrison and Lucas.

"I didn't know he was a reporter," Charlotte said. "He said he was a cop."

"Bastard," Lucas said. "He plays dirty."

"It's not your fault," Harrison said. "We should have anticipated that he'd try to sneak in and prevented it."

"The nurse ran him out." Charlotte ran a hand through her tangled hair. "You think one of those men will try to kill me?"

An awkward tense silence followed.

"You don't have to answer that," Charlotte said. "I guess that's obvious."

"We aren't going to let anything happen to you," Honey said.

"She's right," Lucas agreed.

Harrison cleared his throat. "We'll assign a guard to watch your room while you're here."

"I'm going home as soon as possible," Charlotte said. She hated hospitals.

"I'll stay with you when you come home," Honey offered. "We can have a sleepover."

A footstep, then something rustled. "That's not going to happen, Honey," Harrison said brusquely.

Another awkward silence, then whispering.

"Is something wrong, Honey?" Charlotte asked.

A heartbeat passed. "No, nothing's wrong," Honey said.

"What's going on, Harrison?" Lucas asked.

"Maybe this isn't the time," Honey said in a low whisper.

"For heaven's sake, I may be blind, but I'm not deaf," Charlotte said. "What's wrong, Honey?"

"Nothing's wrong." Honey's hand brushed Charlotte's arm. "I'm pregnant, Charlotte."

A light lifted inside Charlotte. "That's wonderful, Honey. I'm so happy for you."

She tugged Honey into a hug, tears dampening her cheeks. Hers? Honey's? Both.

"Congratulations, brother," Lucas said.

She heard motion and realized the brothers must be hugging.

"Have you told Mom?" Lucas asked.

Harrison shook his head. "You're the first to know."

Honey tucked a strand of Charlotte's hair behind her ear. "I'm sorry, Charlotte, I know this isn't the best time—"

"Shh." Charlotte hugged Honey again "This is wonderful timing. We need good news right now. And a baby…there's nothing more exciting than knowing you're having a little one."

"But you've been hurt—"

"Hush." Charlotte set Honey away from her, felt for her hands and cradled them between her own. "I'm happy for you. You're going to be a great mother."

"She will be," Harrison said. "Just like she's a great wife. But it's my job to protect her."

"You're damn right it is," Charlotte said with conviction. "And if having Honey near me puts her and the baby in danger, then take her someplace far away."

"That's not necessary," Harrison said. "But I do want her on the ranch."

"I'll take the first watch here tonight," Lucas said matter-of-factly.

Fear of the kidnappers slithered through Charlotte. But she wasn't about to show it in front of Honey. "Go home, Honey, please. Take care of yourself and that baby."

Honey hugged her again. "You know I'm here for you, Charlotte."

"I know. But I'd never forgive myself if something happened to you and that baby."

"There's nothing more we can do tonight," Lucas said. "Take your wife home, Harrison. Maybe we'll get a lead in the morning."

Shuffling echoed in the room as the men said goodbye, and Honey pressed her hand against Charlotte's cheek. "Call me if you need me."

Charlotte nodded, although there was no way she'd put her best friend in jeopardy.

Voices and footsteps followed as the three of them filed from the room. Charlotte blinked hard, willing her vision to return. Just a sliver of light. A color.

She always associated colors with moods, feelings, emotions. Blue for relaxing and calming, like the ocean. Red, orange and bright yellow for sunsets and optimism. Green for melancholy.

Black—the darkness she saw now—for emptiness. Fear. Uncertainty.

She tugged the covers over her as if they were a safety net. Honey said to trust Harrison and Lucas. Trust had never been in her vocabulary.

Chapter Seven

Lucas walked Harrison and Honey out into the hallway to leave, then slapped his brother on the back. "Congratulations again. You're lucky, bro. Take care of her and that little Hawk."

Harrison wrapped his arm around his wife's shoulders, tugging her close to him. "Don't doubt it, man. I will."

Honey smiled up at him, her eyes glowing. "I hate to leave Charlotte. She acts tough, but she's scared. More for her students than herself, but I'm worried about her."

"We aren't going to let anything happen to Charlotte," Lucas said, surprised at the fierceness of his own voice. He'd barely met the woman, but there was something about the combination of her vulnerability and strength that roused his admiration and respect.

She also aroused parts of his body he couldn't think about. He had no business noticing how beautiful she was when she was lying in the hospital injured and in danger.

"Let me know if you hear anything," Harrison said.

Lucas nodded. "You do the same." He gestured to Honey. "Now take her home. Mom will never forgive us if we keep the mother of her first grandchild up too late."

Harrison chuckled, and he and Honey walked down the hall, hands linked. Their mother would be ecstatic over the news. She'd grieved for Chrissy for nearly two decades. Although at first she hadn't welcomed Honey, she'd changed. Now she adored Honey and would love that child with all her heart.

A seed of envy sprouted inside Lucas. For years he and his brothers had harbored guilt over Chrissy's disappearance.

It was nice to see that Harrison had found a family of his own.

Lucas had never considered the possibility himself.

Do not go there. You have a case to solve. Charlotte Reacher is part of that case, nothing more.

Why the hell was he thinking about this stuff now? He had to keep his mind on the job. Being focused was imperative to being a successful agent.

The missing girls were counting on him. Lives depended on it.

Determined to stay focused, he scanned the hall to make sure no one was lurking around, waiting to hurt Charlotte. Satisfied it was safe, he stepped to the vending machine, got a cup of coffee, then strode back to Charlotte's room.

When he opened the door, the lights were on, but Charlotte was still, her dark hair fanned across the pillow, her eyes closed, her chest rising slowly with each breath.

She looked peaceful.

But the nightmares would return. If not in her sleep, when she woke up in the morning.

Suddenly Charlotte bolted upright. She clenched the sheets, shaking, her mouth parted in a scream.

"It's all right," he said softly.

Her breathing was erratic. "Honey?"

"She and Harrison left." He brushed his hand over hers. "It's Lucas. I'm right here."

"Lucas?"

"Yes, I'm staying tonight so you can rest." But tomorrow he'd push her to describe the tattoos. A sketch artist might help as well.

She exhaled, then rubbed a hand over her eyes, and his heart went out to her. "I'm sorry," she said in a low voice.

"You have nothing to be sorry about, Charlotte, so don't apologize again. Just lie back and sleep. Hopefully you'll feel better in the morning." Either that, or the drugs the doctor gave her would wear off, and she'd be in pain. Reality would be difficult, especially if her world was pitched in darkness.

"You don't have to stay, Lucas."

"I'm not leaving." He eased her back to rest against the pillows. "Now, go to sleep."

She pulled the covers up over her. Lucas gritted his teeth at the sight of the ugly bruise on her forehead peeking below the edge of the bandage. Anyone who hurt a woman was a monster in his book.

Hurting a child was even worse.

He would find these bastards and make them pay for what they'd done.

Charlotte settled under the blanket and closed her eyes, but sadness lingered on her face.

Damn. She was so beautiful he could barely take his eyes off her. He wanted to wipe out her pain and worry.

He wanted to see her smile.

Oblivious to his thoughts, she winced as she rolled to her side. Her shoulder, the stitches…she was uncomfortable.

But she didn't complain. Instead, she closed her eyes and lay in silence.

He flipped off the overhead light, then settled into the recliner beside her bed to stand guard.

No one was going to get to her tonight. Or any other time.

He'd kill anyone who tried.

CHARLOTTE WOKE THE next morning to the sound of rumbling. For a moment she was disoriented.

The noise again. Soft. Masculine.

Reality rushed back, robbing her of breath. Her students were missing…

The sound—snoring, a man's snoring… Lucas Hawk, Federal agent. He was guarding her because those horrible men wanted to kill her.

She jerked her eyes open, a sliver of light causing her to wince in pain. Then a total void again.

Despair threatened, but she tamped it down.

Still, she felt trapped in this room. Trapped in the dark.

She raked tangled hair from her face and pushed herself to a sitting position. Where were Evie and Mae Lynn and Adrian and Agnes? What had happened to them?

The door squeaked open and footsteps echoed.

Rustling. Then Lucas's voice. "I must have dozed off."

"No problem, Agent Hawk." Haley's voice. "I'm

going to check her vitals and help her get a bath," Haley said. "The doctor will be here in a minute. A vision-rehabilitation therapist is also going to talk with her about handling her vision loss."

Emotion welled in Charlotte's throat. But she couldn't fall apart.

Like it or not, she had to make adjustments.

"I'd like to ask her a few questions," Lucas said. "And maybe get a sketch artist in here."

Footsteps again, coming closer. Then Lucas's masculine scent swirled around her. "Is that all right with you, Charlotte?" Lucas asked.

"Of course. Although I doubt if I can tell you anything more than I did yesterday."

"The analyst at the Bureau sent pics of tattoos similar to what you described. I was hoping we could narrow down the details."

The door opened again, and Charlotte heard more footsteps. "I have breakfast," a cheery female voice said.

Haley cleared her throat. "Give her some time this morning," Haley said to Lucas. "Let her clean up and have something to eat then you can come back."

"All right. But I'll be outside the door."

"Lucas, I'm fine here with the nurse," Charlotte said. "Go home. Get breakfast and a shower."

"I'm not leaving until Deputy Bronson shows up to stand guard."

A reminder that her life was in danger.

"But I'll go get some coffee and be right back."

The door closed behind him, then Haley spoke. "How are you feeling this morning, Charlotte?"

Like she'd been run over by a train. "All right. I'm

ready for coffee and a bath." Then she needed to focus on recovering her memory of the attack.

She had to do something to help find her students before it was too late.

LUCAS GRABBED COFFEE and a sausage biscuit from the café, then checked his messages as he ate. He hadn't meant to fall asleep, but a few hours rest would help today.

Harrison had asked Deputy Bronson to check out the foster parents yesterday so he punched his number.

"Deputy Bronson, it's Agent Hawk," Lucas said when the man answered. "What did you learn about the foster families?"

Bronson made a low sound in his throat, and Lucas realized he must have awakened him. "Let me grab my notes." Noises echoed, then the deputy returned.

"Okay," Bronson said. "Girl named Evie, thirteen, lived with a single woman named Joleen. She's mid-fifties, moving to Florida to be near her grandkids so was about to turn Evie back over to the state. She said Evie behaved at her house, but she'd been in some trouble before. Wouldn't talk about it."

It might not be important, but he'd find out what that was about. "Go on."

"Mae Lynn lived with a couple named Ruth and Philip Cables. According to the couple, Mae Lynn was quiet, withdrawn, depressed. She was a cutter. They thought she needed more help than they could give her and already talked to the social worker about putting her in a residential treatment program."

Poor kid.

"What about the sisters, Adrian and Agnes?"

"Financials indicate that the couple fostering them had money troubles. Husband had been out of work with a herniated disc. Lost his job and disability ran out."

"Were they keeping the girls long-term?"

"They didn't say. The woman seemed concerned about them, said the other foster kids in the house were upset about the kidnapping."

"How many others do they have?"

"Three. All boys," Bronson said.

Maybe the foster father wanted it that way?

THE BATH FELT heavenly and renewed Charlotte's energy. Haley helped her dress in a fresh gown, which made her feel a world better as well.

"Your vitals are normal, and your wounds look good, too," the doctor said. "But it'll take time for you to regain your strength."

"And my vision?"

"Your tests are inconclusive. I'm afraid you'll have to be patient and give your body time for the swelling to go down, then we'll be able to tell more." He patted her shoulder. "Don't give up hope. Meanwhile, our vision therapist is going to talk with you."

"When can I go home?"

A tense pause. "Are you ready to go home? Do you have someone at your place to help you while you recover?"

Charlotte drew in a deep breath. "I live alone, but I'll manage."

Another heartbeat passed. "I realize you're a strong, independent woman," the doctor said. "But you've suffered a trauma and you need to heal both physically and emotionally. Vision loss, even temporary, presents challenges."

She gritted her teeth. "I'm aware of that." Anger at feeling helpless washed over her. She had no idea how she was going to cope. But she couldn't lie in this room in the dark forever.

But like it or not, she was going to need help adjusting. "I'll talk with that therapist about how to handle things at home."

"Good. Work with her and then we'll discuss your release."

Shuffling sounded and he left the room. Charlotte reached for the coffee on the tray that food service had brought, but her hand knocked it over and she yelped as hot coffee spilled onto the table and into her lap.

Frustrated, she pushed away the tray and lifted the sheet from her thighs. Footsteps shuffled, then she recognized Lucas's voice.

"Here, let me help."

Tears burned the backs of her eyelids. "No, I've got it."

But she didn't have it. And the fact that she couldn't have a cup of coffee or eat breakfast without help made her sick inside.

She hadn't relied on anyone but herself for so long. How was she going to live on her own?

Worse, how was she going to help find her students if she was so weak?

EVIE SCOOTED CLOSER to Mae Lynn. She was worried about the girl. She'd stopped crying and drifted into a silent shell. That was worse than the bawling.

Adrian and Agnes were huddled together in the corner on the floor, shell-shocked but alert as if they were waiting for their abductors to return.

Evie had no idea where they were. They'd been traveling for what seemed like hours, over hills and bumps. Once she'd heard water, and felt like they were on a bridge.

In the movies, the people listened for sounds so they could figure out where they were being taken.

But hell, that stupid drug they'd given her had knocked her out and she'd lost too much time. It was so damn dark in here that she didn't even know if it was daytime or nighttime.

She nudged Mae Lynn's arm with her hands. She'd been trying to rip that zip tie off but had only managed to make her wrists bleed. "Stay strong, Mae Lynn," Evie said. "We're going to get out of here."

Mae Lynn didn't budge. Didn't even blink. She just stared into space.

"You know what they're going to do to us, don't you?" Adrian said.

Evie chewed her bottom lip and nodded. "But we're not going to let them. We'll escape."

"How?" Agnes whispered, her voice raw from crying.

"I don't know yet," Evie said. "But we have to stay strong. When the right time comes, we'll find a way." She hesitated. "For now, try to think of what we'll do and where we'll go when we get away."

The girls looked at her as if she was insane. She couldn't blame them. The room or container, wherever they were, was dark and cold and the air felt stale.

But she closed her eyes and imagined Ms. Charlotte's studio. It was the first place where she'd felt happy.

She pictured herself dipping the brush into bright

yellow paint and saw herself painting the sunrise. Orange and red came next, then a garden with beautiful wildflowers in pale lavender and purple. Butterflies fluttered above the flowers and grass, an ocean of colors dancing as the butterflies soared around her face.

She'd never seen this place, but she would survive and find it one day. And nothing would stop her from picking those wildflowers and chasing the butterflies in the garden.

Chapter Eight

The next two days were tense and long for Charlotte. Just as he'd promised, Lucas kept someone posted at her door.

The day before, she worked with a sketch artist to describe the kidnappers for a mock-up to show to the public, but she struggled for details that might help and ended up feeling even more anxious.

Between fatigue, headaches and her frustration over losing her sight, despair pulled at her.

But each time her hope slipped, she imagined Evie singing as she painted, imagined Adrian and Agnes chattering about the horses they wanted to own one day, and Mae Lynn with her big, sad eyes brightening when Charlotte praised her knack for mixing colors to create shades that gave her paintings a layered, thought-provoking look. The girl had talent and didn't know it.

The vision therapist had been teaching her tips on coping without her sight. She'd agreed to come to Charlotte's house, help her organize her rooms so she could function independently and be somewhat self-sufficient.

Charlotte was ready to dive in. Anything to leave the hospital and this room.

Last night, when everything grew quiet, the memories of the attack had haunted her. She'd lain awake for hours, wondering where the girls were and what was happening to them.

She was beginning to think Lucas had overreacted to the media coverage of her survival. She wanted to call off the guards, but he insisted on keeping watch.

Having him near her made her uncomfortable. Nervous.

Not because she feared him, though.

Because his deep, husky voice sounded sexy and triggered visions of Lucas holding her and kissing her.

She silently chastised herself. Why was she lusting after the man when they hadn't found her students?

The door opened, and immediately Lucas's sultry scent wafted to her. Raw. Masculine. Woodsy.

Her heart fluttered. On the heels of her reaction, reality intruded. "Do you have news, Lucas?"

His footfalls came closer. "I'm afraid not. Harrison and his deputy and I have combed the area and searched a half-dozen abandoned warehouses, ranches and farms, but found nothing."

Disappointment mushroomed inside her. "Then the kidnappers may be long gone."

"It's possible," Lucas said, his own voice rough with frustration.

"How about the other agents?" Charlotte said. "You said they were going to the border and to Miami."

"So far, nothing concrete. If this ring is as organized as we believe, they may have paid off officials to help them cross the border."

Charlotte's stomach twisted. The men—and her students—could be in Mexico or off to another country, where they'd never find them. "I wish I could help more."

"You just need to focus on your recovery."

"I am doing that," Charlotte said. "But that's not enough."

"We're all frustrated and worried," Lucas said quietly. "It might not mean anything, but let's talk about your students again. The report on the girl named Evie hinted that she'd been in trouble before, but the court records were sealed. Do you know what happened to her?"

Charlotte swallowed hard. She did know. And he'd asked her this question before, but she'd deflected it each time. She didn't want to break Evie's confidence.

"Why do you think it's important?" she asked.

"It might not be, but we have to consider the possibility that someone in Tumbleweed or one of the foster parents could be involved."

Charlotte massaged her temple where another headache was beginning to pulse. Evie had shot one of her foster parents.

Could he possibly be involved?

LUCAS SENSED THAT Charlotte didn't want to divulge private information about Evie. But they'd reached a dead end, and he had to explore every angle.

For years, his family had believed that Chrissy had been abducted and taken somewhere far away from Tumbleweed. Yet she'd been right outside town all along.

Not that the two situations were the same. This kidnapping was definitely a professional job. It had to be linked to the others.

Still, someone in town could be part of this group. "Charlotte?"

"I don't see how it could be connected," she said.

He waited, letting the silence stretch between them, a technique he'd learned to get people to open up.

"Evie is special to me," Charlotte said, her fingers twisting a strand of hair that draped her shoulder. "She's been through bad times, but she always finds a way to be optimistic. Honestly, bringing her into the group was like a ray of sunshine. Mae Lynn tends to withdraw inside herself. I worry about her more than any of them."

"I understand that you care about them," Lucas said. "But if someone contacted one of the girls on the computer, she may have inadvertently led them to your studio, where they knew a group would be together."

"You checked their computers and social-network sites?" Charlotte asked.

"My analyst is working on it. The people Mae Lynn were staying with didn't have internet access. The couple who were keeping Adrian and Agnes said theirs was limited but allowed us access. So far, the only thing Keenan found was a couple of links to horse camps."

Charlotte pressed her hand to her mouth as if stifling her emotions. "Those girls want to ride more than anything in this world. I just pray we find them and I can help make that dream come true."

Lucas swallowed hard. "We will make that happen," he said, knowing he shouldn't make promises he might not be able to keep. But Charlotte had suffered enough, and he wanted to offer her hope.

Although he was starting to lose it himself.

"Evie's foster mother said Evie didn't spend much

time on the computer. She liked to sit outside and draw most of the time."

"That sounds like Evie," Charlotte said, her voice wistful when she said Evie's name.

"The girl you describe, the optimistic artistic one, doesn't sound like the type who'd have a record. Tell me what happened, Charlotte."

Charlotte inhaled sharply. "Promise me you won't judge her or share this information with anyone else."

Lucas brushed his hand over hers to keep her from fidgeting with her hair again. Seeing her touch it made him want to run his fingers through the long, dark strands.

Damn. He was becoming infatuated with her.

"I promise. I would never do anything to hurt you or one of your students."

She nodded, then released a breath. "The fifth home Evie was placed in was not a good experience. The foster father molested another girl and came after Evie."

Lucas gritted his teeth at the images that flashed behind his eyes.

He'd heard this scenario way too many times.

"Then what happened?"

Charlotte lifted her head as if she was looking at him, but a blank expression darkened her eyes. God, he wished she could see him.

"She defended herself," Charlotte said.

He wasn't sure if he wanted to know the rest of the story. But he had to. "Go on."

"She grabbed the old man's gun and shot him with it," Charlotte said.

Good for her. "Did she kill him?"

"No, but he was injured pretty badly. Blew off part of his leg."

So he wouldn't be chasing any more girls.

"What happened then?"

"The wife called the law. They removed Evie from the home and investigated."

"What was this couple's name?" Lucas asked.

"Willamena and Dick Scoggins."

"How did the investigation play out?"

Charlotte toyed with a strand of her hair. "The other girl backed Evie's story so they were both placed in other homes. The social worker felt horrible and worked to get the charges against Evie dropped and her record sealed."

Dammit, he wouldn't have blamed Evie if she'd killed the monster.

CHARLOTTE HATED THINKING about Evie living in the house with that awful man. Thankfully she'd made it out.

A shudder coursed through her. Only now she'd landed in the hands of men who might be even worse, men who would sell her to others and force her into sex slavery.

The mere idea made bile rise to her throat.

"Please tell me that bastard is in jail," Lucas said.

"No." Disgust left a sour taste in her mouth. "He's in a wheelchair. The prison system didn't have a facility that could house and protect him from other prisoners, so he's free."

She had no sympathy for the man. Anyone who preyed on innocent children and females deserved to be taught a lesson.

"I'm going to talk to him," Lucas said. "The bastard could have wanted revenge against Evie and found a way to steer the kidnappers in her direction."

"I'd hate to think that he was that evil," Charlotte said. "But I suppose it's possible."

A knock sounded and a male voice said, "I'm ready for duty." Deputy Bronson, Charlotte thought.

"Great," Lucas said. "I need to leave for a while."

Charlotte rubbed her hand over her eyes. "I'm being released today."

"Are you ready for that?" Lucas asked.

Was she? No. But she had to face it sometime. "Yes. The doctor has arranged for the vision-rehabilitation therapist to meet me and help me acclimate."

"What time?"

"I don't know yet," Charlotte said. "Sometime late afternoon." She needed to call Honey and ask her to pick up some clothes for her.

"I'll be back to drive you home."

Charlotte tucked a strand of hair behind her ear. "That's not necessary. Deputy Bronson can drive me."

"No, I'll do it."

Lucas's firm voice indicated the discussion was closed.

Charlotte bit her lip. Did she really want Lucas to witness her clumsy attempts to get around in her own home?

Worse, how would she stand being in her house once his scent invaded her space? Already, at night, she'd begun to associate it with comfort. Safety.

She'd even begun to imagine that he wanted to protect her because he cared about her.

That was foolish. She was simply a witness in a case

he needed to solve. He probably hoped that she'd eventually remember something helpful.

She closed her eyes and willed that to be true.

But her mind was an empty void, dark and blank, just like the space in front of her eyes.

LUCAS SHIFTED AND jammed his hands in his pockets. Why didn't Charlotte want him to drive her home? Did she dislike him for some reason?

That thought made his gut churn.

Deputy Bronson would easily handle the task. Yet for some reason, Lucas wanted to do it himself.

He wanted to be the one to protect her. He wanted to be there if she needed someone...

Whoa... What the hell was wrong with him? He knew better than to get involved with a witness in a case he was investigating.

The last two nights when Charlotte had awakened in the throes of nightmares, reliving the shooting/kidnapping, he'd held her in his arms and she'd relaxed against him. He'd told himself he simply wanted to comfort her.

But the hard truth was that he liked holding her. He liked the way she felt against him. He liked the soft, sweet scent of her skin and the way her hair felt when it brushed his cheek, and the whisper of her sultry voice rasping his name as she drifted back to sleep.

Deciding he definitely needed some air and space from Charlotte, he told Bronson he'd be back and headed outside. He phoned Keenan on the way to his car and asked for the address for the Scogginses.

The house was about twenty miles from Dead Man's Bluff.

The summer heat had lifted, the temperature was cooling to the sixties, and the first signs of fall were showing in the leaves as he drove toward the address. Soon the colors would be vibrant reds, oranges and yellows before fading to brown.

Would Charlotte get to see them?

He followed the GPS and turned onto a narrow dirt road that led out to farmland and mountain. Thirty miles later he reached a dilapidated wooden house that sat by a rotting barn. A rusted black pickup was parked beneath a dilapidated carport that was tilting to the right.

He parked and waited until the dust settled around his vehicle before he walked up to the porch. The boards squeaked as he climbed the steps, and he knocked on the screen door.

It took five minutes and knocking three more times before the man's wife answered.

"Mrs. Scoggins," Lucas said as he flashed his badge. "I need to talk to you and your husband."

"What the hell for?" She folded her bony arms and glared at him.

"Five minutes, that's all I'm asking," Lucas said.

She huffed, opened the door and grabbed a cigarette pack as she led him through a run-down kitchen to a living room that reeked of old furniture and dust. Every imaginable surface was covered in dirty clothes, yellowed newspapers, cigarette wrappers and overflowing ashtrays.

The woman lit up, then sank into a rocker beside her husband. Scoggins puffed on his own cigarette from his wheelchair. The man narrowed his eyes and sneered.

Lucas identified himself. "I'm sure you've heard

that four girls were kidnapped from the art studio in Tumbleweed a few days ago."

The old man shrugged. "So. What's that got to do with us?"

"One of the girls was named Evie. She lived with you for a while." He glanced pointedly at the wheelchair. The man's wife stiffened and stubbed the butt of her cigarette into a coffee cup.

The old man snarled. "That's a mean one. Can't say I feel too sorry for her."

Lucas's blood ran cold. He scanned the room for a computer, but the only electronic thing in the room was the television and it was ancient. The phone was an old rotary. "Do you own a cell phone?" Lucas asked.

The couple exchanged confused looks. "You drove out here to ask me if I have a cell phone?" the man snarled.

"Just answer the question. Do you have a cell phone or a computer?"

"Do we look like we do?" Mrs. Scoggins said sarcastically. "Hell, since they took the kids away, we can barely afford to keep the electricity on."

Pure rage shot through Lucas. He hated people who used the system. They took money under the guise of caring for children, yet they spent the money on booze or cigarettes or drugs, not the kids.

"You're lucky you're not in jail." Lucas leaned over the old man in an intimidating stance. "Now, tell me what the hell you know about the human trafficking ring that kidnapped those girls?"

Chapter Nine

"Either leave or I'm calling my lawyer," Mr. Scoggins said sharply.

"That's what cowards like you do," Lucas said. "Hide behind the law when you have no respect for it in the first place."

"Get out," Scoggins shouted.

Lucas folded his arms, then faced the wife. "If you or your husband had anything to do with the kidnapping in Tumbleweed, I'll find out, and you'll pay. But if you cooperate and tell me what you know, I'll see that you get a deal." It wouldn't be a good one, but he'd find some piddly compensation.

"Look at us," Mrs. Scoggins said. "We live in the middle of nowhere. We have no computer or internet. We can't live in town because Dick had to register for that damn stupid sex-offender list. And we sure as hell don't have company. That hateful girl cost us all our friends."

"You and your husband abused innocent children," Lucas said through gritted teeth. "Your behavior is what cost you friends."

"You don't know anything about us," she hissed.

"Oh, yes, I do. I've met others like you. You and your

husband use the foster system to support your habits.
You abused the children, then blamed them. You hated
Evie, and the entire foster system. Maybe you sold out
Evie to get revenge."

She cut her eyes away from him and stared out the
back window.

Scoggins wheeled his chair in front of Lucas. "I told
you to get out, and I meant it."

Lucas glared at him. "I'm leaving, but if I find out
you're lying and that you had something to do with
the abduction in Tumbleweed, I'll be back." He put his
hands on each side of the man's wheelchair and leaned
into his face. "And this time, I'll make sure you're
locked away. This place will look like a resort compared to where you'll be going."

Mrs. Scoggins flinched, but her bastard husband
lifted his chin in a dare. "You ain't got nothing on me."

Lucas dropped a business card on the table in front of
the wife. "Call me if you decide to do the right thing."

With a derisive look, he turned and headed back to
the door.

"If you come back, I'll call the sheriff and tell him
you're harassing us!" Scoggins yelled.

Lucas chuckled to himself. Let him call the sheriff.

Harrison had a baby on the way. He'd always felt responsible for Chrissy, and for Lucas and his two other
brothers.

Just like him, Harrison had no tolerance for predators and pedophiles.

CHARLOTTE RUBBED A finger over the stitches on her forehead, blinking in a futile attempt to alleviate the throb-

bing in her head. She despised taking painkillers. They made her sleepy and put her in a fog.

She needed to be clearheaded, to remember details about the kidnapper.

And she had to concentrate on learning to survive in a sightless world.

She and the vision therapist, Rebecca Cain, had been working for what seemed like hours. Rebecca explained tips that would help her manage her life at home and agreed to meet her there to help her get oriented.

"It will be important to keep your furniture and belongings in a specific place," Rebecca said. "Once you master maneuvering the house on your own, a chair or food item in the wrong place could throw you off."

"I understand," Charlotte said. "Although I like to be creative in my art, I am an organizer."

"Good, that's half the battle." Rebecca paused. "The real work will take place when we get you home. But for now, I want you to visualize the interior of your house. Picture the rooms, the layout, the location of the doors and closets."

Silly for her to close her eyes, but it was a habit she utilized when mentally picturing places, objects and scenes she wanted to paint.

"You're at the front door," Rebecca said. "What do you see?"

This was easy compared to forcing herself to remember the kidnapping. "My friend Honey renovated the house." Charlotte smiled as she remembered the two of them poring over the plans. "She gutted the interior and created an open concept. Hickory floors, a big open room with a living area to one side, a kitchen with an island and bar stools connects to the living area. There's a fireplace on the far wall in the den with a vaulted ceiling."

"And your furniture?" Rebecca asked.

Charlotte could feel the soft leather of the camel-colored sofa. "A sectional sofa with a coffee table made from reclaimed wood. I...whitewashed it myself."

"Sounds lovely," Rebecca said. "Go on."

"I mounted a TV above the fireplace." She paused, emotions fluttering in her chest. "I guess I won't need that."

"You can still listen to it," Rebecca pointed out.

"I like music," Charlotte said. "My Bluetooth speaker connects to my playlists. I usually listen to that instead of the TV anyway."

"Good. Imagine yourself walking through the living area. Where is your bedroom from there?"

"When you enter the house, there's a wide hall that leads to my room and an en suite. A guest bathroom opens to the hall and a guest room. A third room with floor-to-ceiling windows and French doors leading to the backyard lets in natural light. I use that room as my studio. You can see woods and the mountains in the background."

"Sounds beautiful," Rebecca said. "Do you have a back deck or porch?"

"A deck," Charlotte said. "I like to sit outside and watch the sunset in the evening." Her voice cracked. She would miss those sunsets and the view of the mountains and the trees and...the colors. It was fall and soon the leaves would be changing.

She mentally formed a snapshot from past memories but already the image seemed muddy.

Would she eventually forget the subtle nuances and shades of colors?

LUCAS STOPPED BY Harrison's office after he left Scoggins. Too bad the man had survived that gunshot wound. He deserved to be six feet under.

He relayed his conversation with the couple to his brother.

"They do live on the outskirts of town," Harrison said. "Unless they managed to use a computer elsewhere, I don't see how Scoggins could have made contact with the kidnappers."

Unfortunately, he didn't, either. Which pissed him off. He almost wanted the old man to be involved so he could punish him for what he'd done to Evie and that other child.

"How about the library or bookstore?" Lucas asked. "Do they have computers for public use?"

Harrison adjusted his Stetson. "Yes. I'll talk to the owner of the bookstore and Carmella Jones at the library and find out if Scoggins used their internet."

"Better get warrants, so we can search the computers," Lucas said. "If we find something, we sure as hell don't want to have to let that pervert walk."

"True." Harrison stepped aside to call the judge and Lucas walked to Harrison's office. A corkboard above his brother's desk held flyers and pictures from other cases across the state and nation.

The mountains and wilderness areas of Texas provided a perfect refuge for those wanting to live off the grid and hide.

Another board held photos of the missing teens.

The young faces spoke to Lucas and made his heart ache. How many times had they looked at his sister's picture over the years and prayed she was still alive? How many times had he imagined the worst?

Although her life had been taken way too soon, at least Chrissy had had family who cared for her. Family who'd never given up looking for her.

In cases of human trafficking, oftentimes the girls were runaways or homeless and no one missed them enough to report them. Eventually, the search went cold and the cops and feds moved on to other cases.

"I promise you—Evie, Mae Lynn, Adrian and Agnes—that I won't give up. I'll keep looking until we rescue you."

Footsteps echoed behind him, and Harrison appeared. "Getting the warrants. The owner of the bookstore said she hadn't seen Scoggins, but she's pulling records of everyone who used the public computers and will send me the list. I'm still waiting on Carmella to call back about the library."

"We may be chasing false leads," Lucas said, his tone gritty. "But we have to do something."

His phone buzzed. The medical examiner's office. Lucas quickly connected. "Special Agent Hawk."

"I have an ID on the girl you found."

"Who is she?" Lucas asked.

"Her name is Louise Summerton. She's from Sky Falls, fifteen years old."

Sky Falls was a small town about an hour away. "Was she in the system?" Lucas asked, wondering how he'd IDed her so quickly.

"Yes, but not for a crime. Her parents reported her missing a month ago, said she ran off with her boyfriend. They provided a DNA sample when they filed the report."

Lucas heaved a wary breath. The boyfriend could have killed her, meaning she wasn't related to their current case. Or…he could be involved in the trafficking ring somehow. He couldn't discount any possibility.

"What was cause of death?"

"Blunt-force trauma. Looks like she fell and hit her head on a rock."

"Or someone smashed her head with one."

"That's possible, too."

"Gunshot wound?"

"No."

If she'd been shot with the same gun used on Charlotte, they could have linked the cases.

"Did she have defensive wounds? Any DNA under her nails?"

"There were bruises on her wrists."

"Have the parents been notified?"

"Not yet."

"The sheriff and I will handle it," Lucas said. "Maybe the parents can tell us more about this boyfriend."

For all they knew, he could have sold her to this group.

AN HOUR LATER, Lucas and Harrison drove to the Summertons's house. Death notification was one of the worst aspects of the job.

"When is the baby due?" Lucas asked. They both needed a distraction from what they were about to do.

"March. She'll probably be showing soon."

"Are you excited about being a father?"

"Yeah, but I'm a little nervous, too," Harrison admitted.

"That's probably normal," Lucas said.

"Honey's going to be an amazing mother."

His brother's love for his wife was obvious. "You'll

make a great dad, Harrison. God knows you fathered me and Dex and Brayden after Dad left."

Harrison clenched his jaw. "I still can't believe he never contacted us."

"I know. I thought for sure when the news aired about us finding Chrissy that we'd hear something."

Lucas drove through a small neighborhood of older ranch homes and parked in front of a redbrick house overgrown with weeds and bushes.

"Guess that's one mystery that may never be solved," Harrison muttered.

Lucas nodded. When he'd first joined the Bureau, he'd searched for his father, but had turned up nothing. He wished to hell he could sit down and talk with him.

But he had no leads. As time passed, he'd decided either his father was dead or he just didn't want to be found.

He opened his door and climbed out, and he and Harrison walked up to the house. Harrison knocked while Lucas scanned the property. He didn't know what he was looking for, but the job had taught him to always be alert.

A male voice yelled that he was coming, and a minute later, the door opened. A stout-looking man, probably in his forties, stared back at them, a hammer in his hand.

"Mr. Summerton?"

The man's bushy eyebrows formed a unibrow as he frowned. "Yeah."

Harrison was wearing his sheriff's uniform, but he introduced himself anyway, and Lucas did the same.

The man's face paled. "You have news about Louise, don't you?"

Lucas nodded grimly, and the man stepped back and opened the door. "Let me get my wife."

He followed Harrison inside, dread curling in his belly.

Mrs. Summerton appeared, her eyes haunted, as if she already knew what they'd come to tell her.

She fiddled with the collar of her blouse, her hand trembling. "You found our daughter?"

Lucas nodded, and Harrison offered her a sympathetic smile. "Yes, ma'am. I'm sorry," Harrison said.

Her face crumpled, tears filling her eyes as she reached for her husband. He put his arm around her and the two of them walked over to a threadbare sofa and sank onto it, hands clenched together.

Lucas and Harrison followed, giving the couple time to absorb the news.

"Where?" Mr. Summerton finally asked.

"Not too far from Dead Man's Bluff," Harrison said. "We're investigating the kidnapping that happened in Tumbleweed and were checking out abandoned properties. We believe the kidnappers are part of a human-trafficking ring and thought they might be keeping the girls at a ranch or farm in the area until they could move them. That's how we found Louise."

Mrs. Summerton gasped, horror darkening her eyes. "You think they're the ones who took Louise?"

"We don't know," Lucas said quickly. "But we will find out what happened to her, I promise you that."

Tears trickled down the mother's face. "My poor darling… When can we see her?"

Lucas exchanged a look with Harrison, and Harrison spoke. "She's at the medical examiner's office at the moment. I'll let you know when he releases her body so you can make arrangements."

The couple nodded, grief riddling their faces.

Lucas knew they needed time to process the news, but the other girls were still alive. If the cases were related, these people might have information that could help save them.

He cleared his throat. "We understand this is difficult, and we're sorry for your loss." He paused. "But we need to ask you some questions."

"You said that you thought Louise ran off with a boyfriend," Harrison began. "What can you tell us about him?"

Mrs. Summerton swiped at her tears. "I thought we were close, but I didn't even know she had a boyfriend."

"I never believed she'd run off like that," Mr. Summerton mumbled.

Lucas narrowed his eyes, confused. "Then why is it in the report?"

The couple looked at each other as if silently debating how to respond.

"Please tell us what you know," Lucas said.

Footsteps sounded, and a young boy of about ten shuffled into the room, his face drawn. "I told him she ran off."

Mrs. Summerton bit her lip. "This is Roger, Louise's brother."

Lucas angled himself toward the kid. "Roger, why did you think your sister ran off with a boy? Did you see her with him?"

The kid shook his head. "He never came here, but she talked to him on the computer."

Lucas softened his voice. "Is that computer here?"

Roger nodded.

"I need to examine it." Lucas glanced at the parents. "It would be best if we took it with us."

"My daughter was not promiscuous," Mrs. Summerton said. "She was a good girl."

"I'm sure she was," Lucas said. "And I promise that whatever we find on the computer will remain confidential. We are not here to disparage your daughter, only to find out who took her from you."

The couple nodded, and Mr. Summerton gestured for them to follow him. Roger bolted ahead.

Lucas's heart ached for the woman. It had only been a short time since he and his brothers had had to deliver bad news like this to his mother.

They'd thought that having answers would help them heal.

They'd finally found Chrissy's killer.

But it hadn't brought Chrissy back. Just like nothing he could do would bring the Summertons's daughter back to them.

But four other girls' lives were at stake.

And that computer might hold the key to finding out who'd taken them.

Chapter Ten

Lucas followed Roger to Louise's bedroom, where he gestured toward a laptop on an oak desk in the corner. "We're supposed to share, but Louise always used it at night when I went to bed. She didn't want Mom or Dad to know."

Although the boy had obviously taken it over since his sister's disappearance.

"We would like her computer returned when you're finished," Mr. Summerton said from behind him.

Lucas nodded. "Of course." He glanced around the boy's room, noting the basketball posters on the wall along with posters of superheroes. A typical preteen boy's room. Tennis shoes on the floor, dirty clothes piled on top of a hamper, a collection of model airplanes the kid had put together on a shelf above his bed.

"I'd like to see Louise's room," Lucas said.

Harrison exchanged a knowing look with him, and they followed the father to the girl's room. Mrs. Summerton stood in the doorway, tears trailing down her cheeks as she stared at the room.

"I haven't changed a thing since she left," the woman

said, her lower lip quivering. "I kept thinking she'd come back."

Lucas's chest tightened. "I understand," he said quietly. "My family lost my little sister years ago, but her room is still the same." He couldn't stand to go in it, but holding on to Chrissy's things obviously gave his mother comfort, as if part of Chrissy was still with them.

Lucas held the computer to his side while he walked through the room. Harrison went straight to a white wicker desk and checked the top, then inside the drawers.

"What are you looking for?" Mr. Summerton asked.

"Something that might indicate where your daughter met this guy when she left," Harrison said.

Lucas opened the closet door, looking for a treasure box or journal, something private that held the girl's secrets. "Did she have a cell phone?"

Mr. Summerton nodded his head. "Yeah, we finally caved. Only because we thought she might need it for an emergency." He made a sarcastic sound. "Look what good that did."

He stepped from the room and returned with a prepaid phone and handed it to Lucas. The phone was dead. Keenan could retrieve whatever was on it.

Harrison turned, a small diary in his hand. "Mind if we take this? Maybe Louise wrote something about the boy in it."

"She didn't," Mrs. Summerton said, her expression sad. "I read through it. Mostly she talked about how she wanted to get out of this town, away from us."

"That's not uncommon for teenagers," Lucas said, although it was obvious that the girl's statement hurt her mother.

"I know," Mrs. Summerton said. "We weren't perfect, Agent Hawk, but we loved our daughter."

"I don't doubt that," Lucas said. Although if there had been tension within the home, Louise might have written about it in that book or on her computer. You never knew what really went on behind closed doors.

"We'll return the journal, phone and computer when we're finished," Lucas said.

"Just find out who took our little girl from us," Mrs. Summerton said. "He has to pay."

CHARLOTTE TOWEL-DRIED HERSELF in the bathroom. She felt almost human again. Although showering in the dark was daunting, at least she was clean again.

Unfortunately, nothing could wash away the stain of the kidnapping from her mind.

A knock sounded at the bathroom door. "Do you need help?" Honey asked.

Charlotte bit her lower lip. How humbling to think that she might. "No, I've got it. Thanks."

"I hung your clothes on the hook on the back of the bathroom door."

Charlotte had no idea where the towel bar was, so she dropped the towel on the floor by the shower, then felt along the wall until she reached the door and the clothing.

She ran her fingers over the garments in search of tags to determine if they were inside out and where the neck of the shirt fit.

Frustration knotted her insides, but she chastised herself. Coping with her vision loss was nothing compared to what the girls were going through right now. She *would* learn how to manage on her own.

And she wasn't going to whine.

She fumbled with the clothing but managed to finally get dressed. The nurse had given her a toothbrush and toothpaste so she ran her hands over the sink vanity, found them and brushed her teeth. She reached for a cup for water, but couldn't find one, so she used her hand as a cup to rinse.

She felt again for a hand towel and discovered a wall-mounted paper-towel holder and dried her hands.

She searched the sink for a comb or brush. Her hand hit something and knocked it to the floor. Water sloshed onto her feet.

There went the cup of water.

Annoyed, she tried to find the towel to clean it up, but banged her leg on the toilet.

"Charlotte?"

"I'll be out in a minute," she said through gritted teeth. She finally found the towel but was so disoriented she didn't know if she was drying up the water or making it worse.

Finally, she opened the bathroom door. "I spilled a cup of water on the floor," she said, derision lacing her voice.

"Don't sweat it. It's not a big deal." Honey took her hand and led her back to the bed, then disappeared for a minute to clean up the spill. Charlotte fiddled with the bedding as she settled on top of the bed.

A second later, Honey's footsteps padded from the bathroom toward her. She slipped a brush into Charlotte's hand.

"I figured you needed this now."

Charlotte nodded, silently reminding herself not to whine.

"Harrison texted," Honey said as Charlotte brushed her hair. "They found a female body near Dead Man's Bluff."

Charlotte gasped. "No, please…not one of my students."

"No," Honey said quickly. "The medical examiner identified her already. She disappeared about four weeks ago. Her parents thought she ran off with her boyfriend."

"Do they think her death is related to the trafficking ring?" Charlotte asked.

"They don't know yet," Honey said. "They went to talk to the parents."

Fear threatened to paralyze Charlotte. She'd comforted herself by thinking that the kidnappers wouldn't hurt the girls, not if they intended to sell them.

But what if that wasn't their intention?

Or what if one of the girls fought or tried to escape?

If they'd killed one girl, they wouldn't have qualms about killing another.

The girls might be in more danger than she thought.

LUCAS AND HARRISON carried the computer and phone to the lab for analysis. While he watched Keenan run a preliminary search on the phone, Harrison called Honey.

"What can you tell by analyzing her phone?" Lucas asked.

"The same number popped up numerous times, but it belonged to a burner phone as well so there's no way to trace it."

Lucas cursed. "How about the computer?"

Keenan checked Louise's search history and social-media sites.

"She was active on Facebook," Keenan said. "But the stuff she posted is tame." She clicked on the girl's Facebook page and Lucas noted pictures of Louise and her family, then Louise and two other teenagers.

"Who are those girls?" hc asked.

Keenan scrolled through the posts and Louise's friends. "A girl named Phyllis and another named Connie. Looks like they attend school together."

"I need the police reports from when Louise first went missing, I assume the detective or sheriff who investigated spoke with them."

Keenan gestured to another computer, and Lucas used it to access the files while Keenan searchcd for other sites Louise had visited.

Lucas quickly skimmed the file on the initial investigation into Louise's disappearance. The investigating officer had cleared the family of suspicion. He'd also questioned Phyllis and Connie, who both claimed that Louise met a guy online and had become secretive.

Neither knew the boy's name or if they actually hooked up in person.

Lucas rubbed a hand over his face. Could have been a pedophile or stranger, not involved in the trafficking ring. Predators were everywhere.

"I've got an address for a contact Louise made via a teenage singles site," Keenan said. "She and someone who called himself Devon were corresponding for weeks."

Lucas moved over to look at the computer screen with Keenan. "He was flirting with her," Lucas said.

Keenan nodded. "Judging from her posts, Louise

wasn't confident around boys. I'm sure this guy's attention flattered her."

Disgust gnawed at Lucas. If the guy was simply a normal teen looking for a friend, that would be all right, but his gut instinct warned him that wasn't the case.

"Did they meet in person?" Lucas asked.

Keenan tilted her head to the side with a sigh. "They were supposed to meet the day she disappeared."

"This secret boyfriend has to be involved." He'd bet his life that he wasn't a boy, either. That Louise had been lured by a stranger, perhaps one of the trafficking ring.

Keenan nodded. "The IP address leads to an office building in El Paso."

"I'll get someone in El Paso to check it out. Anything else?"

"Where were they supposed to meet?"

"He suggested a teen center about ten miles from the girl's house."

"How was she going to get there? The parents didn't mention that she had a car."

Keenan frowned. "He was supposed to pick her up at the computer café near her house."

"Good God."

"I know," Keenan said softly. "You'd think with all the crazy, scary stories on the news that young girls would be more careful. Unfortunately, teenage hormones overpower common sense."

Especially if a girl was needy or felt homely and was starved for attention.

"Give me the address. I'm going to canvass the people at the café and see if anyone saw or heard anything." He stood, anxious to check out the shop.

Harrison returned and Lucas explained what Keenan had found. "I have a feeling they never made it to the teen club," Lucas said. "But it's on the way to the computer café so we'll stop there first."

CHARLOTTE WAS ANXIOUS to go home. Honey wanted to stay until Harrison and Lucas arrived, but she insisted her friend leave. The last thing she wanted was to put her pregnant friend in danger.

Her head was throbbing so she took a couple of painkillers, then laid back against the pillows and closed her eyes. Images of those men barging into her studio filled her mind. She struggled to see something helpful, but the masks covered their features.

All except for the cold eyes. They were men without a conscience. Men who killed. Who took children and teenagers and sold them like cattle.

Reliving it was hell, but she had to push herself…

She felt the hard whack on her head as the brute slammed the butt of his gun into her forehead. Stars swam and she swayed, clawing to remain upright. Screams filled the air.

One of the men spoke. She struggled to understand, but the gunshot blasted.

Another voice. She was on the floor. Blood soaked her shoulder. Pain splintered through her.

She stared up at the chaos. Her students fighting to get away. Evie running. The brute speaking into a mic on his shirt collar.

She strained to hear what he was saying. Something like Shep… Shet… Shetland…

She sat upright, eyes wide open. Except the darkness greeted her again. Grays and blacks.

She had to focus on the voice. Thick, gravelly, into the mic… Yes, he said Shetland. Like Shetland pony?

Her pulse pounded. What did it mean? Were her memories confused because of the drugs?

No. The man was talking to someone else. Maybe they were discussing where they would meet?

Shetland… Was there a Shetland pony farm somewhere nearby? If so, the girls could be there…

Chapter Eleven

Lucas and Harrison scanned the area surrounding the teen center as they parked. On the drive, Lucas phoned the deputy director, who'd assigned another agent to check out the warehouse in El Paso.

The teen center was a freestanding concrete structure with art deco-style sketches on the sides that had probably been painted by the teens.

A strip shopping center sat behind it, housing a pizza joint, ice cream parlor, karate studio and western mercantile.

"Someone could easily have parked in the shopping center and scoped out the teens," Lucas said as they walked up to the entrance.

"Yeah, but in the last three instances, groups were taken. Louise supposedly disappeared by herself."

True. Lucas reached for the door and opened it. Noises echoed through the front entry as they entered. Signs indicated a gym, basketball courts, a swimming pool and exercise equipment. Rooms were designated for teen classes, including dance, aerobics, Zumba and spinning. A sign pointed down the hall toward a rec room for special events, a snack area, a media center with a big-screen TV and a stereo system.

Lucas introduced himself and Harrison to the receptionist. He flashed a photograph of Louise.

"We need to know if this girl was a member," Lucas said. "Her name is Louise Summerton."

The young woman studied the picture then shook her head. "I don't remember her, but let me check our members' and visitors' lists."

Harrison looked through the glass windows at the pool area, where several teens swam laps.

"I don't have her name on either list," the young woman said.

"Do you mind if we talk to some of the other teens?" Lucas asked. "Maybe one of them remembers her."

"Sure. But why are you asking about her?"

Lucas lowered his voice so as not to create alarm. "Because she disappeared a few weeks ago. According to her computer, she planned to meet a guy here."

The young woman's eyes widened. "That's awful."

"Have there been any problems at the center?" Lucas asked.

"What do you mean?"

"Any unwelcome guests? Fights between teens? Perhaps an older man stopping by or watching from outside?"

Fear darkened the woman's face. "No one has reported anything like that."

Harrison glanced at the camera in the corner. A wall-mounted TV displayed various areas of the center, along with the entrances and exits.

"Can we look at your security tapes?"

"Let me call the manager." She punched a button and paged a man named Jordan Lansing. Seconds later, a tall, broad-shouldered man in shorts and a T-shirt appeared. He looked like a football coach, tough and big, and greeted them with a friendly smile.

The young woman quickly explained the reason for their questions, and the man's expression changed to concern. "You think this girl disappeared from the teen center?"

Lucas shrugged. "We don't know yet. According to her social media, she planned to come here with someone she met online." Lucas showed the man a photograph of Louise. "Do you recall seeing her?"

An odd look passed over the man's face, then he shook his head. "No, but she could have come on one of my days off."

Lucas pulled up the calendar on his phone to show him the date the girl went missing. "I'd like to see the security tapes from this date."

Harrison cleared his throat. "While you're doing that, I'll talk to some of the other teens. Maybe one of them knew the girl."

The receptionist called one of the teen counselors to the front to escort Harrison through the center while the director led Lucas to a security office, introduced him to a guard named Juan Perez and explained what he needed.

"We have cameras on all the entrances and exits, along with the stairwells," Perez said.

Lucas was impressed that they were trying to make the center as safe as possible. The guard scrolled through the tapes and located the one for the day Louise disappeared.

He, the guard and Lansing studied the footage,

watching as teens came and went. A group of girls had congregated for a swimming class, but Louise wasn't among them. A few teenage boys gawked at the girls and made crude comments about them before disappearing into the locker room.

But no one stuck out as suspicious.

After scrolling through the tape twice, then searching through other tapes from that same week, Lucas sighed. "She wasn't here. He must have met up with her at the coffee shop." Or in the parking lot or on the street nearby.

He gave the director his card and asked them to call if anything suspicious turned up, then went to meet Harrison.

His phone buzzed just as he joined Harrison outside the teen center. The hospital.

His breath caught. He hoped to hell Charlotte was all right.

Nerves on edge, he punched Connect and said hello. "Lucas?"

"Charlotte, is everything okay?"

"Yes, but I may have remembered something."

His pulse jumped.

"It might not be anything, but I was thinking about when the men burst in… One of them spoke into a mic attached to the collar of his shirt."

"Coordinating with the team," Lucas said.

"That's what I thought. I couldn't hear everything they were saying, but I think he used the word *Shetland*."

Lucas frowned. "Like Shetland pony?"

"Yes. I know it sounds crazy, but I was wondering if

there's a Shetland pony farm nearby. Maybe they took the girls there."

Hope budded inside Lucas. "I'll find out. And, Charlotte?"

"Yes?"

"Thanks. Harrison and I have one more stop to make and I'll come to the hospital to drive you home."

"Just find the girls," Charlotte said. "I can get another ride."

He knew damn well she could. But he wanted to take her home.

Wanted to make sure she got settled into her house and that she was safe tonight.

CHARLOTTE SAT ON the edge of the bed, hands knotted as she waited on Lucas. For once she was grateful that she didn't normally wear makeup. At least she didn't have to worry that she'd smeared mascara across her nose or cheeks.

She repeatedly racked her brain for other details about the kidnappers. If she had her sight back, she'd research Shetland pony farms herself, but until she adapted her house and computer and her lifestyle to accommodate her vision loss, she was at the mercy of others.

A knock sounded at the door and she tensed, then listened for it to open.

"Charlotte, it's Lucas."

Relief surged through her. Deputy Bronson was nice, but there was something about Lucas's deep voice that soothed her soul.

She fiddled with her hair, smoothing it down. "Yes?"

"Are you ready to go home?" Lucas asked.

She turned toward his voice, wishing she could see his expression, but she had to rely on memory.

His deep-set brown eyes had looked serious in the photograph, intense, just as she imagined them to be now. His cleft chin, thick five-o'clock shadow, and gruff voice added to his masculinity. She was surprised he wasn't taken.

Then again, Honey had confided that the Hawk men harbored guilt over their little sister's disappearance and had remained single, devoting themselves to law enforcement. Until Harrison had fallen in love with Honey, that is.

"Charlotte?" Lucas's footsteps came closer. "Did the doctor release you?"

She slipped off the bed and stood, steadying herself by placing one hand on the edge of the mattress. "Yes. I'm ready to go." She straightened her spine, searching for courage.

"The nurse is bringing a wheelchair," Lucas said.

Charlotte lifted her chin. "I don't need it."

"Whoa." Lucas's voice gentled as he touched her arm. "It's hospital policy. Every patient leaves in a chair."

She suddenly felt silly. "Of course." She should have known that. But her pride smarted.

Another knock, then Haley's voice. "I'm here to take you downstairs."

Charlotte nodded. The vision therapist planned to meet her at the house, after Charlotte arrived and called her. All she had to do was make it to the car and get in her house, then she could start learning how to lead her life.

Haley guided her to the wheelchair and she sank

into it. She held her head high as Haley rolled her down the hall toward the elevator, certain people were staring at her.

Noises echoed around her. A laugh. Voices. A loud beep. A shrill screech.

Someone was crying.

With every strange voice and sound, the reality of her situation struck her. She was in the dark, didn't understand what was going on, who was talking, how far they were from the elevator or what floor she was on, or if someone was watching her.

For all she knew, the kidnappers could be waiting at her house to ambush her, and she would have no clue.

LUCAS WAS TEMPTED to help Charlotte into the car, but he fought his instinct. Charlotte was fiercely independent. Leaning on others would be difficult for her.

He understood the feeling. He would hate it if he was in her shoes.

Still, part of him wanted to sweep her into his arms, hold her and take care of her every need.

She fumbled for the seat belt, and he kept his hands by his sides to keep from fastening it for her. The nurse offered him an encouraging smile and he returned it, but the moment the door closed and he was alone with Charlotte, nerves set in.

"I appreciate you driving me," she said as she clicked the seat belt.

"No problem." He shifted into gear and drove from the hospital parking lot.

"I live in that neighborhood Honey developed," Charlotte said.

"Honey texted me the address."

Charlotte angled herself toward the window as if she could see out, and his heart ached for her. "What time is it?" she asked softly.

He checked the clock. "About six o'clock," he said. "Almost dinnertime. Why don't I stop and pick up something?"

A heartbeat of silence passed, tense and raw with emotions she obviously wanted to suppress.

"I guess that would be good. I like to cook, but… that's not possible at the moment."

He couldn't help himself. He reached out and covered her hand with his. "Give it time. You've just suffered a terrible trauma, both physically and emotionally."

"I will cook again," she said stubbornly. "Now, talk to me."

Lucas smiled at her spunk, then relayed his visit to the teen center. "Are you familiar with that facility or the director, Jordan Lansing?"

It had occurred to him that Lansing could possibly be involved. But he'd seemed like a nice man, interested in helping teens and protecting them.

Hell, he'd been fooled before though.

What better setup for preying on young girls than a facility where they gathered in droves?

"I've heard of it and Lansing," Charlotte said. "The program is legit. God knows, the teens need it. Lansing is a good guy. He lost a child of his own and is trying to help save others."

So he could most likely strike Lansing off the suspect list.

He explained about the email exchange between Louise and the alleged boy who wanted to meet up with her. "We stopped by the computer café, though, and no one recognized Louise or remembered anyone suspicious hanging around."

"You think it was a setup to lure her away so the boy could take her?" Charlotte said.

"It's possible. We're airing her photo on the news with her story. Hopefully if someone saw something, they'll speak up."

"I keep wondering what's happening to the girls," Charlotte said. "If the same group killed Louise, how do we know they'll keep the girls alive?"

Lucas opened his mouth to offer her encouragement, but a gunshot pierced the front right side.

"Get down!" he shouted.

She screamed, and he shoved her head to her lap as he swung the car onto the shoulder.

The glass shattered as another bullet hit the passenger window.

Chapter Twelve

Charlotte covered her head with her hands, her body jerking as Lucas swerved off the road. The brakes squealed, and the tires were grinding as they bounced along the shoulder of the road, then he straightened so quickly that she was thrown against the console.

Another bullet pinged the car, and Lucas cursed and sped up.

"Lucas?"

"Just stay down. I'll lose the son of a bitch."

Another quick jerk of the car, and she banged her elbow on the door. She raked shattered glass from her hair, her breathing choppy as she fought panic. The car sped up, flying and bouncing across rugged terrain.

She clung to the seat as he swung the car around and screeched to a stop.

"What are you doing?" she cried.

"I want to find out who this SOB is." He stroked her hair. "Listen to me, Charlotte. We're at the edge of a ravine, so do not get out of the car. Do you hear me?"

Her head was buried in her arms, but she lifted it slightly and nodded.

"Stay down and don't move until I return."

She blinked, fighting fear. "Where are you going?"

"I parked behind a boulder. I'm going to fight back."

She gulped back a scream of protest as the car door slammed, and she was left alone in the dark.

LUCAS CURSED. HE'D managed to get ahead of the damn shooter, but the bastard was coming for them. Dust spewed to the right where a dark Jeep sped down the dirt road.

Lucas ducked behind the boulder, then quickly glanced back to make sure Charlotte was still in the car. The door was closed. Thank God she'd listened.

Wiping perspiration from his brow with his sleeve, he pulled his gun and took aim.

The Jeep barreled around the corner, then slowed as if searching for them. Lucas counted the seconds, waiting until the car was close enough to hit, then fired. The bullet skimmed the top of the Jeep, and the driver wove to the side. Damn. The windows were tinted. He couldn't see inside.

A second later, the Jeep spun around and headed straight toward the boulder, where he was hiding. Lucas cursed, then fired another shot and another as it roared toward his vehicle.

His bullet hit the windshield and pierced the glass, making the driver swerve to the left. He hit rocks and dust, and gravel flew in a cloud around the Jeep. But it didn't stop.

The driver straightened, then accelerated and roared over the terrain, cutting to the right to go around the boulder. It was heading straight toward his car. Dammit, was he going to push it over the edge with Charlotte inside?

He raced to the right and fired, sending bullets into the driver's window. The driver jerked sideways. The Jeep went into a skid and raced over the edge of the ravine.

Lucas jogged to the edge and looked down. The Jeep flew nose-first, slamming into rocks along the side, then careened into the rocks below. A loud crash reverberated in the air, then the gas tank exploded.

Lucas scanned the area surrounding the Jeep in case the shooter managed to escape. Nothing.

Flames burst into the air, smoke billowing as orange, red and yellow streaked the sky.

Another explosion and the rest of the vehicle turned into a ball of fire. Flames engulfed the Jeep, and smoke curled into the sky in a gray fog.

Satisfied the shooter couldn't have survived, he jogged back to his car. One glance confirmed that Charlotte remained inside.

His heart pounded as he opened the car door. "It's me, everything's all right."

She looked shell-shocked and shaken. Tears tracked her cheeks and her pale face looked haunted.

"Where is he?" she asked in a choked voice.

Lucas slid into the driver's seat, then pulled her up against him. "Dead. He crashed over the ravine."

Her body trembled against him, and he wrapped his arms around her, stroked her hair and held her.

Dammit, it could have been them going over that ravine. Charlotte could have been shot.

"I won't let anything happen to you," he whispered. "They won't get you, Charlotte."

Not as long as he had a breath left in his body.

CHARLOTTE LEANED INTO LUCAS, grateful he was alive and they were safe. But the reality that someone had tried to kill them—her—sank in, driving fear deeply within her.

She wished she could stop shaking, but she was trembling from the inside out.

Lucas rubbed circles over her back, a comforting gesture that she savored. He could have been killed trying to protect her.

But he hadn't hesitated.

It's his job. Nothing personal.

The reminder made her take a deep breath. Still, for a moment she laid her hand against his chest, drinking in his warmth and strength.

Lucas was the most honorable man she'd ever known. No wonder Honey had fallen in love with his brother and his family.

"Are you okay?" he murmured against her ear.

She nodded, then lifted her head. She wished she could look into his eyes, see what he was thinking. If he pitied her or…found her attractive.

She silently chastised herself. It didn't matter if he did. He had a job to do and she refused to be a demanding, needy female.

"Did you get a look at him?" she asked as she leaned back against the seat.

His breath rushed out. "No, the windows were tinted. Once it went over the edge and crashed, he didn't get out."

He'd probably died on impact. Either that, or he was trapped and burning in his car.

A shiver rippled through her. She hated to think

about anyone suffering. But if he was one of the kid-nappers, he deserved what he'd gotten.

"I need to call CSI," Lucas said.

Charlotte nodded. "Go ahead. I'm fine now." Although she wasn't fine and they both knew it.

But she was alive, and for now, that was all that mattered. The girls were going to need her once they were found.

THE NEXT HOUR dragged by. Lucas helped Charlotte from the car and led her to a group of rocks to sit while the CSI team processed the car.

They gathered the bullet casings from the side, and the one on the floorboard that had shattered the window. The breeze picked up, swirling dust and leaves across the terrain and blowing Charlotte's hair around her face.

He couldn't help but stare at her for a moment. She was so damn beautiful. Even with her porcelain skin discolored with bruises and the stitches evident on her forehead, her long black hair framed delicate features that accentuated high cheekbones, a small button nose and eyes that were so blue they reminded him of the gulf.

She thumbed her hair back from her face, and lifted her head to the wind. His chest clenched. Charlotte was an artist.

It must be especially painful for her not to be able to see colors.

A car engine rumbled, and Lucas glanced up as his brothers approached. He'd called Dexter and asked him to bring one of the ranch vehicles for him to drive.

Dexter glanced at the smoke billowing in the sky,

and then at Charlotte. Brayden strode to the edge of the ravine, then whistled as he returned.

"No way the shooter survived that."

"I just hope there's enough left for the ME to make an identification. We need every bit of help we can get on this case."

Dexter gestured toward Charlotte. "How's she holding up?"

"She's actually been amazing," Lucas said, wishing he'd phrased his comment differently when his brothers graced him with curious looks.

"I mean, she's strong," Lucas said.

Dexter simply nodded, but Brayden gave him a sideways grin. "Honey raves about how much time and love Charlotte put into that art studio. A damn shame those men shot up the inside."

"It can be fixed," Lucas said, making a mental note to talk to Honey about it. Although first he'd have to ask Charlotte if she wanted to return to the space. The trauma might drive her to close the studio or move away.

"Thanks for the SUV," Lucas said.

"You want us to stick around?" Brayden asked.

Lucas shook his head. "No need, CSI has this."

Dexter elbowed him. "Let us know how we can help."

Lucas nodded. "I will. Thanks."

His phone buzzed just as they drove away. Keenan. He quickly connected. "Agent Hawk."

"I've been researching the Shetland reference," Keenan said "There's a Shetland pony farm about fifty miles from Tumbleweed."

Lucas's pulse jumped. "Send me the coordinates. I'll check it out."

He hurried toward Charlotte and told her about the call. "I'll drop you at home then drive out there. Let me make sure someone can stand guard."

"That's crazy," Charlotte said. "You don't need to waste time driving me home. I'll ride with you to the property."

Lucas hesitated. They'd already had one close call today. What if they drove to this farm and found the kidnappers on the premises?

NERVES RATTLED THROUGH CHARLOTTE. She wanted to go home and curl up in her bed.

But if Lucas had a lead, they had to follow it. "Please, Lucas. I'll stay in the car. I don't want you to waste time if there's a chance you might catch these guys and find my students."

A tense heartbeat passed. "I promised to keep you safe. I'm not sure having you ride with me out there will accomplish that."

"Don't treat me like an invalid," Charlotte snapped. "The fact that one of the ring shot at us means the group hasn't moved too far. Maybe they're at that ranch."

Another tense silence. "That's true." He helped her up, and she stood, brushing at her jeans. "But if it looks like someone is there, you have to promise to stay in the car. I can't protect you and chase them if they try to escape or fight back."

"I'll do whatever you say," Charlotte said with a shiver. "Let's just go."

"All right."

The scent of smoke filled the air, a reminder that they'd barely escaped death today.

She curled her fingers around Lucas's arm, slowly checking her footing as she walked.

"My brothers dropped off one of the ranch SUVs for me to drive," Lucas said as he coaxed her into the passenger seat.

She fumbled for the seat belt, cursing her clumsiness as her fingers brushed Lucas's.

"I've got it," he said. "Just try and relax."

Relax? How could she possibly do that knowing someone had just tried to kill her?

LATE AFTERNOON SHADOWS painted the road with gray lines as Lucas drove toward the Shetland pony ranch. According to the text Keenan had sent, the business had folded a little over a year ago.

Abandoned and remote, it would make the perfect place to house the kidnap victims. It was also close enough to Tumbleweed for the kidnappers to come back for Charlotte.

Charlotte lapsed into a strained silence as he drove, the tension between them palpable. He admired her strength and resilience.

But she had to be afraid.

The desert land gave way to farmland and dry brush, a testament to the remote location of the ranch. Charlotte's eyes were closed, although her fingers worried the hem of her T-shirt in a nervous gesture.

"What brought you to Tumbleweed?" Lucas asked, striving to help her relax.

"Honey's renovation project," Charlotte said. "I saw a write-up about her plans and was drawn to her sketches. I drove out to meet her the next day."

"Honey has revived this town," Lucas said, remembering how badly the town had treated her as a child. His mother had been one of the worst. Although now she loved Honey like a daughter.

She would probably like Charlotte, too.

Where had thought come from?

Worried he was getting too close to Charlotte, he clamped his mouth shut and allowed the silence to stand between them for the next half hour. He could not get personal with Charlotte.

She was a victim, a witness, for God's sake.

She needed him to be clearheaded and do his job.

The sign for the ranch slipped into view, the wooden post tilting sideways.

"Where are we?" she asked.

"We passed Dead Man's Bluff and turned west. We're pulling down the drive to the ranch now. The ranch went out of business a while back." His gut churned as he surveyed the land. "Damn, it's not only deserted, but all the buildings on the property have also been torn down."

He parked, punched Keenan's number, put her on speaker and explained that the place was deserted. "Keenan, Shetland is also a type of cattle. See if there are any Shetland cattle farms around."

"Okay, hang on."

The sound of keys clicking echoed in the background. She returned a few moments later. "There is a Shetland cattle ranch about forty miles from where you are now. The property's in foreclosure. I'm sending you the coordinates."

"Thanks, Keenan." He ended the call, checked the text, then turned around and headed toward the cattle ranch. If it was in foreclosure, the ranch was probably abandoned now. A good place for the kidnappers to hide.

"Shetland cattle?" Charlotte said. "I've heard of those. They're working cattle."

"Right." Just like the girls would be made to work. Lucas grimaced, and they fell into a tense silence as he drove. Miles of farmland spread in front of him, then the houses became more sparse.

He found the road leading to the Shetland cattle ranch and turned, following it toward the main hub of the ranch.

This property looked deserted as well, although some of the outbuildings and stable fencing remained.

He scanned the land in search of a vehicle or any sign that the kidnappers were around, but nothing stuck out.

Two run-down barns and a large stable occupied the front of the property, and a dilapidated farmhouse sat on a hill.

Abandoned farm equipment had been left rusting in the pasture, and a dented pickup without wheels was parked in the bushes.

Charlotte seemed to sense they were getting close. "Is anyone here?"

"It doesn't appear so. But they could have locked the girls in the barn or somewhere on the property until they returned."

Charlotte shivered. "How can people treat each other so cruelly?"

"I ask myself that all the time."

He cut the engine, then laid his hand over Charlotte's. "I'm going to lock the door then search the property. I need you to stay inside." He took her hand and placed it over the horn. "If you hear anything, make some noise and I'll come running. And stay down."

Charlotte sucked in a breath and nodded, and he squeezed her hand to reassure her, then grabbed a flashlight from the dash and climbed out.

He squared his shoulders, senses alert as he scanned the ranch again. No activity. Still, he held his gun at the ready as he strode to the barn door and peered inside.

A stench hit him—something was dead inside.

He clenched his gun, praying it wasn't one of Charlotte's students.

Chapter Thirteen

Lucas yanked a handkerchief from his pocket and pressed it over his mouth and nose as he entered. The interior space was dark. Stalls on both sides of a center walkway appeared empty, but he had to check them out to make sure.

Dammit, he had to find the source of that stench.

Shining his light along the floor and into the stalls, he found rotting hay and animal feces. A dead coyote lay in the last stall. Flies and insects swarmed the space. He swatted them away with his hand, gagging at the intensity of the foul odor.

Satisfied no one was being held inside, he exited the back of the barn and noticed a storage shed behind it. He scanned the area. No cars or signs of life.

Using his flashlight, he checked the ground for footprints and tire marks, and spotted boot prints near the storage shed.

He aimed the flashlight over the boot prints and followed a trail of them that led to a graveled area where the men might have parked.

Heart racing, he hurried to the door of the storage shed, expecting to see a lock, but there wasn't one.

If the girls were here, the men would probably have padlocked the door.

Disappointment flared inside him. He pushed open the door then swung the flashlight in a wide arc across the interior. Metal shelves hung on one side of the building while a large metal cage sat on the other.

Bile rose to his throat as he approached it. This cage was big enough to hold a large animal. Or…several small humans.

Anger hardened his jaw, and he aimed the light on the floor of the cage to examine it. It was dirty and blood was smeared on one corner. A broken fingernail sat by the blood.

He lifted the flashlight and studied the wall that the cage was jutted up to.

Several scratches marred the surface, scratches made by a nail or some other small metal object.

In the top corner there were more indentations. This time the scratches formed two words.

Help us.

CHARLOTTE JUMPED AT the sound of the wind blowing. The vision therapist said that her other senses would become more acute, that she'd notice sounds and smells that she normally didn't pay attention to.

Or maybe it was just her nerves. Knowing someone had tried to kill her and that she was alone and helpless in the car made her strain for sounds of a car or footsteps or the kidnappers' voices…or the girls' voices screaming.

Hopefully with joy that Lucas had found them.

But only the shrill whistle of the wind filled the awkward silence. She tried to calm herself by imagining the fall leaves fluttering to the ground in the breeze. Red and yellow and orange would dot the land and create a rainbow of colors.

Footsteps crunched on gravel. Outside the car.

She froze, holding her breath. Lucas? Or could one of the kidnappers have been hiding somewhere on this ranch and snuck up to kill her?

A gentle tap at the window and then the car door was opening. "It's me, Lucas," he said softly.

Relief surged through her, and her breath rushed out. "Did you find anything?"

"They aren't here," Lucas said. "But they may have been." He slid into the seat beside her. "I found a cage where someone was held," he said, his voice laced with disgust. "Someone scratched the wall beside the cage and spelled 'Help us.'"

Charlotte bit back a cry, her heart aching.

"I'm calling CSI," Lucas said. "There might be DNA in the cage. Then at least we'll know if it was your students in there or someone else."

The image of a cage holding humans struck Charlotte with a wave of nausea. She'd known sex trafficking was a huge problem. But like most people, she'd felt it at a distance.

Now that it had touched her life personally, she not only wanted to find her students, but she also wanted to do something to prevent it from happening to others.

WHILE LUCAS WAITED on CSI to arrive, he phoned the deputy director. "Any word from Hoover or the agent in El Paso?"

"Hoover hasn't turned up anything concrete. And the agent in El Paso said that office space was empty."

"Any sign the kidnappers or others involved in the trafficking ring had been there?" Lucas asked.

"It was cleaned out. Not a desk or chair left, or any electronics."

"Sounds like professionals who didn't want to leave any trace of themselves behind." Lucas spotted the CSI van approaching. "Keep me posted." He ended the call, then spoke to Charlotte. "The CSI team is here. I'll be back in a minute."

She nodded and leaned her head against the headrest. Lucas hurried over to the team and explained what he'd found. "Look for traces of blood and DNA. I want to verify who was held in that cage."

Lucas pointed out the storage shed where he'd found the plea for help and took photos of it for his own references. The CSI team dispersed to search for evidence and process the scene.

Then he joined Charlotte in the SUV. "They're processing the property now. I'll take you home."

She toyed with the end of her hair as he drove, a nervous gesture that made him want to reach out and hold her hand and calm her.

But he clenched the steering wheel instead. Touching her stirred feelings inside him.

Feelings he didn't have time for.

"I'm supposed to let the vision therapist know when I arrive home," Charlotte said. "But I don't have my cell phone. I left it on the corner desk in the front room at the studio."

"CSI took it for evidence," Lucas said. "We'll stop and buy you a burner one until you get yours back."

She dug in her pocket and removed a business card.

"Here's the number for the therapist. Do you mind calling her?"

The edge to her voice told him how difficult it was for her to ask for help. "Of course not. By the way, Charlotte, I arranged for a crime-scene cleanup crew to take care of your studio after CSI finished in there." Her certainly hadn't wanted her to return to that bloody scene.

"I hadn't thought about the studio." A shudder rippled through her as if she was reliving the shooting and kidnapping. "I hope we can salvage the girls' art."

"When you're rested and up to it, I'll go in with you and we can assess the damage."

Charlotte's lower lip quivered. "I'm not sure what difference it'll make. If my sight doesn't return, I don't know what I'll do. I won't be able to teach art anymore."

Lucas's chest squeezed. She was facing a lot of challenges. "There are other mediums you could try. How about sculpting?"

Charlotte pressed her lips into a thin line. "I don't know. We'll see."

The fatigue of her surgery must have worn on her, or maybe she simply couldn't deal with the thought of losing her art, because she closed her eyes and drifted to sleep. The sound of her quiet breathing soothed his own anxiety as the vehicle ate the miles back to town.

If this trafficking ring was international, as he suspected, sooner or later something had to break.

He stopped at a convenience store and bought her a burner phone, keeping his eye on the vehicle from inside as he paid.

She was still asleep when he climbed inside and started the engine. Although even in sleep, turmoil strained her features, and the bruise on her forehead looked stark.

The quiet strength emanating from her twisted his insides, though, and he phoned the vision therapist and left a message that Charlotte would be home soon.

An hour later, Charlotte roused from sleep as he pulled into her driveway. "We're here."

She heaved a wary breath, her body stiffening as if she dreaded going inside.

"One step at a time," he said softly. "Just take it one step at a time."

She nodded and reached for the door.

CHARLOTTE STOOD BY the SUV, nerves fluttering through her. She'd parked in her drive a hundred times, but today she was disoriented.

This is your home. You helped build it, you know the layout. You've made happy memories here.

She'd loved watching the sunset over the back deck, had hung ferns on the front porch. There were three, or was it four, steps leading to the front porch?

The idea of finding her way to the front door suddenly seemed daunting.

"The vision-rehabilitation therapist will be here in a few minutes." Lucas lifted her hand and placed it on his arm. "Are you ready to go in?"

Was she? No.

But she would learn to adapt.

"Yes."

He patted her hand, and she curled her fingers around his arm, her stomach fluttering as she felt the muscles in his biceps. He guided her to the porch, pointing out a loose rock and an uneven patch of grass as they walked.

"Your house is beautiful," Lucas said. "Did you choose the blue paint color?"

Charlotte smiled as she remembered the conversation with Honey. She wanted a pale blue like the ocean. "Yes. Blue is my favorite color."

"I like the porch and porch swing," Lucas said. "It looks very homey."

"Honey did a great job remodeling the place," Charlotte said. "There's a back deck, too. A good place to watch the sunset."

Except now she wouldn't be able to see the sun setting or rising.

It didn't matter. All that mattered was finding Evie, Mae Lynn, Agnes and Adrian.

"We're at the steps," Lucas said.

Charlotte nodded, carefully feeling her way. One step. Two. Three.

"Last one," Lucas said.

"You must have done this before," she said, appreciating his patience.

"No. If I was in your shoes, I'd be pissed right now."

"I am," she said. "But it's taking all my energy not to fall apart." And not to fall all over him. But she bit back that thought.

He chuckled. "I'll try to keep you from falling."

"Don't worry about me," Charlotte said, one hand on the rail. "Just find my students and bring them home safely."

"I'll do my best." He paused and she realized they were at the door. Harrison had given Honey her purse from the studio, and Honey had brought it to the hospital so Charlotte fished out her keys and handed them to Lucas.

The wind picked up, ruffling her hair and stirring the wind chimes. They tinkled and clanged, music to her ears. She imagined leaves raining down to the ground, the fall colors swirling.

The sound of the door opening dragged her from her thoughts. Charlotte froze, listening for other sounds inside, determined to orient herself. The entryway led to an open-concept living room with an island and kitchen decorated in blues and whites. She'd positioned her sectional sofa facing the fireplace. French doors led to the porch.

"It's nice," Lucas said. "You have a talent with color. I like the abstract on the wall above the sofa. Did you paint it?"

"I did, I was excited over finally having a home of my own."

"It shows in the splashes of color," Lucas said.

She gave a sarcastic laugh. "Now everything is black."

A tense heartbeat passed and she regretted her comment. She hadn't meant to complain.

"Don't give up hope," Lucas murmured. "The doctor said it'll take time for your body to heal."

Outside, a car engine rumbled. "Who is that?"

"Probably the vision therapist," Lucas said. "I'll let her in."

"Thanks." She envisioned the furniture placement and felt along the wall until her leg bumped the sofa. She raked her fingers along the edge until she found her favorite spot.

She sank into the cushions, exhausted and terrified of her new life.

LUCAS'S PHONE BUZZED just as the vision-rehabilitation therapist entered the house. She was a brunette with a warm smile named Rebecca.

He escorted her inside and over to the sofa, where Charlotte was sitting. "I need to take a call. I'll be on the front porch."

"We'll be fine. We have a lot of work to do to make Charlotte feel at home here again," Rebecca said.

The strain on Charlotte's face made his gut clench. "Let me know if you need anything."

She nodded and quickly turned to Charlotte.

He checked the message. Keenan.

Hoping she had a lead, he stepped outside and quickly returned her call.

"I traced an IP address from a computer to the Summerton girl's laptop," Keenan said.

"Who does it belong to?" Lucas asked.

"The computer leads to a banker in Tumbleweed. Fifty-year-old Herman Stanley." She paused. "Lucas, Charlotte Reacher got the loan for her studio at that bank."

Lucas's mind raced. The banker in town had access to money, knew the comings and goings of the business leaders in town. Knew Charlotte personally. He'd also know how to hide money if he was being paid to provide information to the trafficking ring.

He checked his watch. The bank would be closed now. "Send me his home address."

"It's on its way."

They ended the call, then Lucas phoned Harrison to fill him in. "Bronson can guard Charlotte while we talk to Stanley," Harrison said.

Lucas agreed. If Stanley had intentionally set up Charlotte's studio for attack, he would make sure he paid big-time.

Chapter Fourteen

Lucas rushed to tell Charlotte and her therapist he needed to follow a lead. They were counting the steps from the sofa to the kitchen.

A pang went through him. Charlotte shouldn't be suffering like this.

"I have to check out a lead, Charlotte." He turned to Rebecca. "How long will you be here?"

"A couple of hours," Rebecca said. "We're making progress."

"Bronson is on his way over to watch the house," he said. "Stay inside, Charlotte, and keep away from the windows."

The therapist looked alarmed for a moment. "I'll close all the shutters."

"Let me check all the locks on the windows first." Lucas combed through the house, checking the security aspects. Harrison had said that Honey installed dead bolts on all the doors in her houses. She'd wanted to add a security system but had left that decision up to the owners.

He examined the windows and made sure each one was locked, then returned to the living room. "You should have a security system installed right away, Charlotte. Do you want me to set it up?"

A tense second. "I suppose that would help."

Lucas left his card on the table by the front door. "If you need anything, Rebecca, call me."

Rebecca handed him a business card with her number on it as well. "Don't worry, Agent Hawk. I'll take care of her."

"Charge up her phone and put my number in so she can easily find it."

"I will. And I'll make sure it's voice-activated so she can call whoever she wants," Rebecca said.

"Deputy Bronson should be here any minute. I'll wait outside until he arrives."

He stepped out front just as Bronson pulled up. "Thanks for coming, Deputy."

The deputy gave a quick look around the property. "How's the access in the rear?"

"Back deck with a door to the inside. All the windows are locked and so is the dead bolt on the back door. I'm going to arrange for a security system to be installed."

Lucas jumped in his SUV and drove to the sheriff's office to pick up Harrison. "I have the warrant," Harrison said as he climbed in the passenger side.

Lucas plugged the address into his GPS and drove through town, then followed the road to the lake where the banker lived.

"What do you know about Herman Stanley?" Lucas asked.

Harrison grimaced. "He's a shrewd businessman. He practically ran the home owners in Lower Tumbleweed into foreclosure. Collected on all the debts and made himself a small fortune."

"Did he give Honey a hard time when she bought the property?"

Harrison's mouth tilted into a smile. "Yeah, he wanted her to work through him, but she didn't trust him. She found backing from an investor she'd worked with in Austin."

"Good for her."

Harrison nodded, his smile fading into a grim line as Lucas wove down the tree-lined drive to Stanley's estate home. The house was a large brick Georgian complete with columns, a circular drive and ranchland that stretched for miles and miles. A swimming pool and tennis court were visible from the driveway.

A black Cadillac sat in the drive along with a white Mercedes and a sleek gray BMW convertible.

Lucas parked in the circular drive, and he and Harrison walked to the door. A loud chime echoed through the house and exterior as Harrison punched the doorbell.

Night had descended and the sky was dark with storm clouds, obliterating the stars and moon. Looking up at the black night made him think of Charlotte and how difficult it would be to live in the dark.

The door opened, and a short, rail-thin lady in a maid's uniform answered the door. "Stanley residence. How may I help you?"

Harrison gestured to his badge, and Lucas flashed his credentials. "We need to talk to Mr. Stanley."

"I'm afraid he's not here. Do you want me to give him a message?"

"Where is he?" Lucas asked.

The woman narrowed her eyes. "In Austin on business."

Harrison pushed the warrant in her hands. "We need to look around."

The maid gasped. "What's going on?"

"Hilda," Lucas said as he read her name tag, "we have reason to believe Mr. Stanley may be involved in the disappearance of a young girl named Louise Summerton, and possibly the kidnapping that occurred in Tumbleweed. Do you know anything about that?"

The woman's eyes widened, and she shook her head vigorously.

"If you know something about his business and the missing girls, tell us. If you don't, and we find out you lied to us, you'll go to jail as an accomplice."

CHARLOTTE FORCED HERSELF to concentrate on the tips Rebecca offered. They mapped out the interior of her house, giving her a mental picture of where everything was placed. Rebecca provided her with a cane to help her maneuver the rooms, and she counted steps from each piece of furniture to the next.

Together she and Rebecca organized her bathroom toiletries so she could locate her toothbrush, toothpaste, hairbrush and towels.

Even the simplest task seemed overwhelming. She'd made so many mistakes already that her head was spinning. The first thing she'd done when she tried to maneuver the kitchen was break a glass.

Rebecca suggested plastic glasses at first to help prevent breakage, and Charlotte agreed.

"You're doing great, Charlotte," Rebecca said. "I realize this may be overwhelming at first. You can't learn everything in a day, but you've made a lot of progress."

Charlotte sank onto the sofa with a cup of hot tea Rebecca had made for her and sipped it. "I used to love to cook, but I don't think I'll ever feel comfortable using the stove or oven. What if I catch something on fire?"

"One step at a time," Rebecca said. "I was told that your sight loss might be temporary. You may not need to learn to use the oven, but if you do, we'll master it."

"You're so positive," Charlotte said. "How long have you been doing this?"

"About five years. But I grew up with a blind sister, so I already understood the complications of living without sight and how important it is to keep your environment in order. You'll have to tell people not to move your furniture or your remote or the contents of your cabinets. Once, I wasn't thinking and left a tube of antibiotic ointment on the bathroom counter. My sister mistook it for toothpaste. I felt terrible afterward."

"You sound like an amazing sister," Charlotte said.

"My sister is the amazing one. Not only is she self-sufficient, she teaches visually impaired children."

"It must be nice to have a close family," Charlotte said.

"It is." Rebecca hesitated. "How about you? Do you have parents or siblings close by?"

Charlotte shook her head. "No, I grew up in the system. That's the reason I chose to work with the teenagers through my art studio."

Another awkward moment passed. "I'm sorry about what happened. But it sounds like the sheriff and Agent Hawk are doing everything they can to find the man who shot you and abducted your students."

"They are." Charlotte took another sip of her tea. She just hoped it was enough.

"Tomorrow I'll come back and help you organize your cabinets and pantry. We can also tag your clothing so you can pair items that match."

Charlotte nodded. "Maybe I should just buy twenty white T-shirts and jeans so I don't have to worry about confusing them."

Rebecca laughed softly. "That's an idea. But judging from the gorgeous artwork on your walls and your dishes, I think you like color."

"What difference will it make if I can't see it?"

Rebecca's breathing rattled in the air, and the sofa cushion dipped as the woman sat down next to her. Charlotte startled when Rebecca took her hand, then placed it over her heart. "You've been through a terrible ordeal and a shock, Charlotte. But you are still the same loving, kind person who likes art and colors and who devoted her life to those teenagers. Nothing can change that. Not the kidnapping or the shooting. Not even the loss of your sight." She paused. "So keep fighting, okay?"

Charlotte's throat clogged with emotion. She bit down on her lip, hating that she was on the verge of tears.

"Promise me," Rebecca said.

Charlotte laid her free hand over Rebecca's and nodded. "I promise."

"Good. Now, you have to be exhausted. So let's get your room and you prepared for the night before I leave. I can also set up your coffeepot so you can make coffee in the morning."

Nerves mingled with relief. Lucas had said he'd stay

over, but she didn't want to depend on him. She wanted to do things for herself. "Thank you. I'd appreciate it."

They spent the next half hour practicing how she would manage coffee and breakfast, then Rebecca helped her think through her clothing arrangement so she could find her pajamas, and clothing for the next day.

"It helps that you're already organized," Rebecca told her.

"I guess it's a control thing," Charlotte said. Although now she felt totally out of control and she didn't like it.

Rebecca's phone buzzed. Charlotte heard her step away, then she returned a moment later. "I have to go."

"Is everything okay?"

"Yes. I promised my sister I'd pick her up." She squeezed Charlotte's hand again. "You're going to be okay. I promise. I'll make sure that deputy is still outside."

Charlotte forced a smile, but inside her nerves kicked in. Rebecca's footsteps echoed across the wood floor, then the front door shut. The sudden silence enveloped her, igniting her fears.

Don't panic. Remember what she taught you.

Exhaustion tugged at her, and she took a deep breath and decided to put on her pajamas. Outside, an engine rumbled. Rebecca leaving.

She used her cane and counted the steps to her bathroom, then washed her face and looked where she knew the mirror hung. How many times as a kid had she stared at that port-wine birthmark and wished it gone?

Now it was gone, but since she couldn't see herself, it didn't matter.

But the scars and ugly taunts she'd received from kids still reverberated in her head. Those taunts had shaped her. Changed her.

Just like the shooting and her vision loss would.

Determined to stay strong, she stretched out on her bed to rest while she waited for Lucas to return.

Seconds later, she fell into a fitful sleep. The men were storming her studio, the girls were screaming, she was trying to save them but she was bleeding...

She jerked awake, her breathing erratic, then heard a noise outside. A car?

No...a loud thump. Then low voices.

Voices... Men's voices. Not the deputy's or Lucas's or Harrison's.

Terrified, she reached for her phone. Rebecca had set certain numbers on speed dial for her, so she pressed the number for the deputy. A second later, the phone rang. Once. Twice. Three times.

He wasn't answering.

Another noise.

Heart pounding, she clutched her phone to her chest. She had to call Lucas. But first she needed to hide.

She and Rebecca had practiced how to get to her den and the kitchen. But the best place to hide was the attic.

She gripped her cane in one hand and slid off the bed, then counted the steps to the hall.

Fear pushed her forward, and she felt along the wall for the attic door. Hands shaking, she fumbled with the lock.

Another noise. This time out back. Someone was trying to get in.

She bit back a scream, then threw open the door and felt for the wall and steps. Adrenaline kicked in, and she closed the door behind her and locked it from the inside, then crawled up the stairs to hide.

LUCAS SEARCHED THE banker's office while Harrison strode to the man's bedroom. He combed through desk drawers, looking at files Stanley had brought home. Dozens of business files, portfolios, stock and investment information and personal records.

He flipped through one file and noted several large cash deposits. Stock investments and dividends didn't pay out in cash.

Where had the money come from?

The man's laptop was missing. He probably had it with him. But he had a desktop. Password-protected.

Dammit. He texted Keenan to get a tech analyst to come out, open it and search the man's browser history and files. If he had pictures of girls/conquests on the computer, they could nail him.

Hoping he had hard copies, something that would confirm they were on the right track, he dug into the file cabinet and combed through dozens of folders.

Dammit, no incriminating pictures.

That didn't mean he didn't have some. The man hadn't made his fortune because he was stupid. He obviously knew how to hide what he was doing.

Determined not to leave without searching every corner, he opened the closet and scrounged through file boxes. He found information on the property Honey had bought back after Stanley had foreclosed on it. Just as he'd suspected, Stanley hadn't given the families any leniency. He'd forced them into taking out second mortgages and upped the interest rates so high that the owners couldn't possibly make their payments.

Harrison strode down the steps, boots clicking. "Did you find anything?"

"Just a boatload of financial material. You?"

"So far nothing that links him to the trafficking ring."

"I called the Bureau to send someone out to get into his computer. We'll have to find him and confiscate his laptop as well." He checked his watch, suddenly uneasy. "Let me call Bronson and check on Charlotte."

He punched Bronson's number, and let it ring but it rolled to voice mail. The hair on the back of his neck prickled. Something was wrong.

He called Charlotte's number, but she didn't answer. Panic stabbed at him, and he tried Bronson again.

"Something wrong?" Harrison asked.

"No one's answering. I have to go."

"I'll wait here on the tech team."

Lucas nodded and hurried toward the door. The maid was hovering over the glass figurines in the curio in the foyer, dusting them, her eyes flickering with nerves.

He didn't bother to stop and talk to her. He jogged to his car, jumped in and sped toward Charlotte's.

Fear threatened to consume him as he barreled down the drive and onto the road leading back to town. He needed a damn siren, but the ranch SUV didn't have one.

He blew his horn and flashed his lights at traffic, waving the drivers to move aside as he careened around them and flew through town. By the time he reached Charlotte's home, terror choked him.

He slowed as he approached her house, scanning the property. No cars in sight. Maybe someone had parked in the woods down the road.

He swerved into the driveway, his headlights illuminating the front bushes and porch. A shadow caught his eye. Movement.

To the right.

Someone was out there. Bronson?

No, this guy was wearing all black and he was skulking along the side of the house.

Rage and fear seized him. He pulled his weapon, threw the SUV into Park and jumped out.

Chapter Fifteen

Where the hell was Bronson?

Lucas glanced in the deputy's car, but Bronson wasn't inside. He scanned left and right, then spotted him lying face down near the porch, his body half-hidden by the bushes.

He stooped down and eased toward him, then felt for a pulse.

Low but thready.

He quickly checked for injuries—a nasty gash on the back of his head. He turned over his body. No bullet wounds.

The bushes rustled to the right, and he spotted the shadow again. Men were going through the back door.

He punched 911, then gave them the address and shoved his phone in his pocket. Slowly he inched around the side of the house, careful not to make noise. If he could catch these guys alive, he could force them to tell him where the girls were.

Inside the house, a light glowed in the kitchen, but no other lights were on. Did Charlotte know there were men outside? Was she in the kitchen?

He inched closer to the kitchen window, but Rebecca

had closed the shutters and it was difficult to see inside. Charlotte could already be in bed.

He mentally recalled the layout of the house. The master bedroom was on the opposite side of the house from the kitchen.

A noise made him quicken his pace. One of the men was inside.

Dammit.

He closed the distance to the back deck. The door to the inside was ajar. The dead bolt hadn't stopped the bastard or even slowed him down.

He eased toward the steps, but leaves rustled behind him and the barrel of a gun dug into his back. "You're not going to stop us," a man growled.

Lucas froze. Dead, he couldn't save Charlotte. But he sure as hell didn't intend to let this bastard stop him.

"Leave her alone. She can't identify you."

"Orders. We never leave witnesses behind."

Lucas didn't hesitate. He spun around, jerked the gun into the air and slammed his fist into the man's stomach. Rock-hard. Muscular.

He might be ex-military.

The gun went off, the bullet hitting the porch rail. The man fought back, threw his leg up and kicked Lucas in the knees. Pain knifed through him, and he dropped to the porch floor, struggling for air.

Dammit, he didn't have time to waste. His assailant lowered the gun again and aimed it at Lucas. He quickly rolled to the side to dodge the bullet then raised his own weapon and fired.

The bullet caught the man in the chest. His eyes widened as he realized he'd been hit, then he charged toward Lucas with a rage-filled roar.

Lucas fired again, then again. A bullet pierced the man dead center in his heart. Blood gushed and the man collapsed on the porch then tumbled down the steps and landed in the bushes.

Lucas kept his eyes trained on the bastard as he grabbed the man's weapon and tucked it in his jeans.

There was still one man inside. He couldn't let him hurt Charlotte.

Gritting his teeth at the throbbing in his left knee, he grabbed the railing and dragged himself up then staggered through the door. Footsteps echoed from the back room. Charlotte's bedroom.

A wave of cold fear washed over Lucas.

He swallowed back a growl and crept down the hall toward the intruder.

CHARLOTTE BURROWED BENEATH the quilts in the trunk she'd stored in the attic, fear nearly paralyzing her. The sound of gunshots reverberated in her ears.

Had the intruder shot the deputy?

Footsteps pounded below. Then someone was trying to open the attic door.

She held her breath and clenched the quilt edge, digging her fingers into the soft material. More footsteps. A hard slamming sound—someone kicking in the door?

She pressed her fist to her mouth to stifle a cry. Where was the deputy? Was he alive?

Another noise. In the kitchen, not the attic stairs. Were there two of them?

Her lungs squeezed for air. God help her.

She didn't want to die.

Footsteps, the stairs squeaked. Then a voice.

"Stop right there."

Her pulse jumped. Lucas. He was here to save her.

A gunshot sounded. She jumped, choking on a sob, then forced herself to lie still. A bang, then a grunt. Then a body hit the floor.

Lucas shouted something, then she heard banging and grunting as if the men were scuffling. Tumbling down the stairs.

She closed her eyes and prayed Lucas won the fight.

LUCAS SLAMMED HIS fist into the man's jaw, then his stomach. This brute was bigger than the other one. Muscular, too, with a thick neck like a linebacker. Although his face was covered with a black mask.

He wanted to see his face.

But the brute knocked Lucas backward. Lucas lost his footing and tumbled down the stairs. His gun hit the floor a few feet away. The man pulled his weapon, but Lucas lurched to his feet and ducked sideways. He reached for this gun, but the man came after him. Lucas caught him around the knees and knocked him back onto the steps. The man grunted and raised his gun, but Lucas slammed his wrist and sent the gun flying onto the steps.

They traded blows, rolling across the floor and fighting to retrieve Lucas's gun. The intruder kicked Lucas in the stomach with his boot, but Lucas rolled toward his weapon and snatched it. He spun around and aimed, but the man had disappeared.

Footsteps pounded, then the back door slammed. Lucas lurched to his feet and gave chase. He ran through the hall to the kitchen, then outside, but the sound of a motorcycle engine came from the woods behind the house.

He raced down the porch steps, aimed his gun and fired at the motorcycle as it ripped across the backyard toward the street. Panting, he chased it, firing again and again.

But the man was too fast, and the motorcycle sped onto the road and disappeared.

He wanted to go after it. But Charlotte was inside somewhere. At least he didn't think the men had gotten to her.

Heart hammering, he glanced over at the dead man then raced inside. "Charlotte, it's me, Lucas. He's gone!"

He combed through the downstairs, searched her bedroom and closet and her studio, then made his way back to the attic.

Fear crowded his chest as he entered the stairwell again. "Charlotte, it's Lucas. Are you in the attic?"

He eased up the steps, praying she was safe, his heart in his throat. She had to be okay.

Only there had been four men who'd stormed into her studio. And no telling how many more were involved in the trafficking ring.

What if another one had gotten to her before he'd arrived?

CHARLOTTE TREMBLED AS she cowered inside the trunk, her instincts warning her not to move or make a sound. The world was a blur, the darkness a tunnel that sucked her into its endless vortex.

She shoved her fist against her mouth again, choking back a sob. A squeak of the stairs. The wind outside banged against the roof. The upstairs door into the attic rattled.

"Charlotte, I'm here, it's Lucas! The intruders are gone. Are you in there?"

Relief whooshed through her, and she heaved a ragged breath. Perspiration trickled down the side of her cheek, as tears she didn't know she'd shed blended with the moisture.

"Charlotte, please tell me you're all right."

Lucas. His voice, deep and comforting. Worried.

She had to pull herself together.

"I'm here," she called, although her voice was muffled in the fabric of the quilts. Realizing he couldn't hear her, she pawed her way through the covers, pushed open the lid of the trunk and gasped for air as she climbed out of it.

She was dizzy. Disoriented. Which way was the door?

"Charlotte?"

"I'm in here," she said, her voice raw with emotion. "I locked the door. Give me a minute to find it."

"I can pick the lock or break the door if you want."

She sniffed and wiped her sweating palms on the legs of her pajamas. "No, I'm coming. Just talk to me so I can find the door."

She forced herself to stand still and listen, not to run blindly through the space. An antique dresser she'd planned to refinish stood on the wall near the dormer window, a few boxes of art supplies stacked beside it. The trunk…she'd left it on the opposite side of the dormer window facing the door.

Feeling along the edge of the trunk for the lock, she swung her hands out to feel her way. She'd dropped her cane somewhere on the stairs.

"Charlotte, I'm right here," Lucas said, his voice gruff. "Talk to me."

"I'm okay," she said, although that was a lie. She'd

been terrified she was going to die and never see him or her students again.

"You were smart to hide," he said in a low voice.

"What about the deputy?" she asked as she found the wall and inched along beside it toward his voice.

"I called an ambulance. He was unconscious but breathing, a knock on the head but no gunshot."

His voice was so reassuring that her breathing began to steady, and she picked up her pace.

"The ambulance should be here soon, Charlotte. Are you hurt?"

"No," she said, grateful her voice didn't completely falter. She stumbled over an object on the floor and reached for something to steady herself.

"Charlotte?"

"I'm fine." She straightened her spine and bumped the wall, then realized she was at the door. Her breath whooshed out. She felt for the lock and turned it, then pulled at the knob.

"I've got it," Lucas said. "Step back."

Still trembling from the ordeal, she inched to the side. A second later, the door opened and Lucas's masculine scent filled the air. Her head swam with relief, and she reached out to touch him.

He instantly drew her into his arms, her breathing erratic. She fell against his chest and drank in his warmth and strength as he wrapped his arms around her and held her close.

Lucas raked his hands over Charlotte's back, desperate to know that she was unharmed. "Did they hurt you?" he said against her hair.

She shook her head, one hand flat on his chest as if

she needed to hold on to him to stand up. She was trembling, her breathing erratic, her fear bleeding into his.

"I heard a scuffle outside and called the deputy, but he didn't answer so I decided to hide."

"I'm glad you did," he murmured, hugging her closer, so close he felt her breasts rising and falling against his chest. Unable to help himself, he stroked her back, then lifted one hand and threaded his fingers through her hair. Needing to see that she was unharmed, he tilted her head back and studied her face.

She was terrified, but holding on to her courage. Her eyes were blank as she struggled to see him. His heart ached for her. For him.

He wanted to look into her eyes and see if she felt the same chemistry he felt. He was drawn to her like he'd never been drawn to another woman.

His breath whispered out. She murmured his name. "I want to see you," she said so softly he almost didn't understand her.

Then he realized what she was asking.

He cradled her hands in his then lifted them to touch his face. A smile curved her mouth, and she ran her fingers up the side of his face to touch his hair. He held his breath while she planted her fingers in it, stroking the top, then down the sides.

"I keep it short for the job," he said, feeling awkward as hell.

She nodded, then traced her fingers over his forehead, over his eyes and nose. She inhaled sharply, his own breath quickening as she traced her fingers over his cheek. His breath caught as she touched his lips with one finger.

She wet her lower lip with her tongue, stirring every

male primal instinct within him, and he couldn't resist.

He cupped her face in his hands, lowered his mouth and closed his lips over hers.

Chapter Sixteen

Charlotte clung to Lucas, savoring the feel of his lips against hers. It had been a long time since she'd been held by a man or kissed like this.

Maybe she never had.

Because Lucas's kiss felt hungry, needy, as if he wanted her. But she felt safe at the same time.

He was gentle, as if he thought she was a delicate flower whose petals would fall off if he became too aggressive.

That gentleness made her want more.

She slid her arms around his neck and pulled him closer, deepening the kiss, silently telling him with her mouth and her body that she wanted him.

He stroked her hair with one hand, glided his other hand to her waist and coaxed her into the vee of his thighs. With a whisper of her name, he teased her lips apart, then plunged his tongue into her mouth, stirring erotic sensations to flutter in her stomach.

Passion ignited inside her, making her feel tingly inside, and she moaned softly. She'd simply wanted to feel his face, know the planes and angles of his bone structure, the contours of his jaw, and…just to be close to him.

No, she needed this. Wanted this and more.

She could have died at the hands of those awful men. So could he have. But he'd rushed into danger to protect her.

Another deep kiss left her breathless, then he trailed kisses along her neck and ear. She wanted more. Wanted to feel his bare chest and his body heavy on top of her. Wanted to feel her legs sliding against his, his thick sex stroking her and giving her pleasure.

A siren's wail burst into the night, jarring her from the euphoria of his arms. The deputy was outside, hurt. Her students were still missing, terrified, fighting for their lives.

She and Lucas didn't have time to indulge in sating their selfish desires.

She lowered her hands just as he eased away from her.

"I'm sorry, Charlotte, that shouldn't have happened."

Instantly, she tensed and stepped backward. She wished she could see his face, read his expression, but that was impossible. She had to rely on the tone of his voice and it was laced with guilt.

She didn't want to talk about it, though. "You'd better see about the deputy."

He took her hand, but she jerked away.

"I'm just going to help you down the stairs," he said gruffly.

Heat climbed the back of her neck. She should have realized that. But she was too shaken and confused to think rationally. Worse, her body still tingled, ached for his touch.

She took a deep breath, held out her hand and ignored the desire rippling through her as she allowed him to lead her down the stairs.

LUCAS SILENTLY CURSED himself for losing control. He shouldn't have kissed Charlotte.

Dammit, he wanted her. Wanted to touch and taste every inch of her. Wanted to make her *his*.

That sounded barbaric, even in his own mind. But hell, it was true.

He'd never wanted a woman like he wanted Charlotte. And a first kiss had never affected him the way that one had.

Her hand trembled as she placed it in his, and he cursed himself again. She'd been frightened and vulnerable and he'd taken advantage of the moment.

He wouldn't do it again.

She deserved better. A protector who didn't act on the lust that was driving him crazy.

He forced a calmness into his voice as they left the attic. An image of her, terrified and feeling her way up those stairs, taunted him, rousing his anger.

One man had escaped. One was dead outside.

Dead men didn't talk. But hopefully they could learn something from his body. An ID might lead them to the man's background, his contacts, how he'd gotten involved in this trafficking ring.

And to who else was involved.

The siren wailed closer, lights flickering in the front yard as it screeched to a stop.

"We're in the hall now," he told Charlotte.

"I'll wait on the sofa while you take care of things."

He nodded, then realized she couldn't see him and guided her to the couch. She felt for the cushions, then sank onto it, and he rushed to the front door to meet the ambulance.

Deputy Bronson was dragging himself up from the ground as Lucas made it onto the porch. He hurried down the steps to him.

The deputy looked confused, and was rubbing the back of his head. "Dammit, they ambushed me. Is Charlotte all right?"

"She is," Lucas said. "How about you?"

"Took a knock to the head. But my pride hurts more than it does."

Lucas guided him over to the steps. "Take it easy, the ambulance is here."

Two medics, one female and one male, approached. "What do we have?"

"Deputy has a head injury." Lucas gestured toward the back of the house. "There's also a dead man out back. He tried to break in and kill the woman who lives here."

The CSI team rolled down the drive, and two investigators jumped from the van.

Lucas explained the situation to the CSI team. One member had worked the crime scene at Charlotte's studio, so he was familiar with the case.

The female medic stooped down to assess Bronson's injury then take his vitals. The CSI team followed Lucas inside the house, and he introduced them to Charlotte. "They'll process the house. Is that all right?"

"Do whatever you need to do to catch these guys and end this," Charlotte said. "I'll wait here."

Lucas wanted to sit with her and comfort her, but there was a dead body out back.

"One of you can start in here, and the other can

follow me to the dead man." He gestured toward the hall and rear door. "When I arrived, two figures were sneaking around the house in the bushes. They came around the side of the house and entered the back door. I caught one of the men and we fought, and I shot him. The other man came inside to search for Charlotte. My guess is that he checked the downstairs then found the attic door, broke it and then started up to get her. That's where we tangled." He paused, angry at himself. "Unfortunately, he escaped."

Lucas nodded while the younger CSI started at the back door, dusting for prints and searching for forensics.

The second medic followed Lucas to the bushes, where the dead man was. Lucas and the CSI snapped photographs, then Lucas rolled the man to his back and removed his mask.

He should have looked like a monster. This man had nearly killed Charlotte. He'd taken innocent girls and done God knows what.

Death had been too quick and easy for him.

But he looked like someone Lucas might see on the street.

Lucas snapped pictures of his face, then his body, then dug in the pockets of his black jacket for an ID. Nothing inside. No wallet or ID of any kind.

"Look for identification when you search the property. The one who escaped left on a motorcycle," Lucas said. "If they didn't come together, this guy's motorcycle may still be in the woods. His ID might be there." Still, he sent photos to Keenan to start searching DMV records and facial-recognition software for the dead man's identity.

A car engine rumbled from the front. "Must be the ME," Lucas said. "I'll let him know what we've got."

"Is DEPUTY BRONSON all right?" Charlotte asked as Lucas returned from the outside.

"His pride is hurt more than anything," Lucas said. "He took a blow to the head, but he'll be okay. The medics are going to transport him to the ER for stitches."

"Did he see the men's faces?"

"No, they wore masks and jumped him from behind. I removed the mask from the man I killed. I didn't recognize him, and he had no ID on him, so I sent a picture to our analysts. They'll search databases and use facial-recognition software to ID him."

Lucas had killed a man to save her life. That thought disturbed her. Although the despicable man had kidnapped her four students and planned to sell them, so she tamped down the guilt.

"Are you okay, Lucas?"

A heartbeat passed. "Yes, he took the brunt of the fight. So did his partner before he escaped."

"That's not what I mean. You killed a man. Does that bother you?"

Another heartbeat passed, then footsteps echoed on the wood floor. They stopped in front of her, his masculine scene enveloping her.

She'd never realized how sexy a man could smell.

She felt dizzy, light-headed, from breathing him in.

The sofa cushion dipped as he sat down beside her. Then he took her hands in his.

That simple touch and connection made her want to kiss him again.

But he'd obviously regretted the kiss, so she wouldn't instigate one herself.

"I don't like to take a life, Charlotte. But I came to terms with the fact that sometimes it's a necessary part of my job. This man was evil. He and his group hurt you and four innocent teenagers. He would have killed you if I hadn't killed him first."

She swallowed hard. "I know. But I'm still sorry it came to that."

He murmured that he understood. "I do regret not being able to take him alive," Lucas said. "But only because I might have been able to force him to give us information about the girls."

She squeezed his hands. "What happens now?"

"CSI is processing the crime scene."

She flinched. These animals had tainted her studio and her home.

"Hopefully we'll identify the man I shot and that will give us a lead on the group. The one who escaped left on a motorcycle. We searched the woods and found the second one, so we'll process it as well. I plan to get a security system installed in your house tomorrow."

"I appreciate that," Charlotte said. If Lucas used someone he trusted, she could trust them, too.

"All right, I'll make a call." He released a weary breath. "I'm sure you're exhausted. It's nearly midnight and you were just released from the hospital."

A shudder coursed through Charlotte. She'd been plagued by nightmares since the abduction.

There was no way she could sleep in her house tonight.

Lucas felt Charlotte's shudder rip through him. She was holding up amazingly well.

But at some point, everything was going to hit her. It always did.

Then victims crashed hard.

Right now, she was hanging on to the hope of finding the girls. But each day they were missing meant the chance of finding them alive or unharmed decreased.

"It's going to take the team a while to finish up. I'm sorry, but there'll be fingerprint dust on surfaces. I'll call a cleanup crew to come in the morning."

Charlotte bit her bottom lip and gave a little nod. Her strained expression indicated how she felt about her home being invaded, first by two monsters and now by crime investigators.

This was the home she'd built. Her colorful art pieces hung on the walls. Her furniture and decor was light and airy, bright with the hope of a future.

Now it had been tainted.

He wished he could change what had happened. But all he could do was help her through it.

"I'm taking you to my place tonight," Lucas said. "The kidnappers know where you live. They might come back."

She shivered, emotions darkening her face. "I could stay in a hotel."

"No." The thought of her being in a strange room alone didn't sit well in his gut.

"Our ranch, Hawk's Landing, is secure. No one will think to look for you there."

"I don't want to endanger your family," Charlotte said. "Especially since Honey is pregnant."

"My cabin is on the opposite side of the ranch," Lucas said. "No one will get to you with me there."

He'd die first.

Chapter Seventeen

Charlotte felt disoriented and displaced as Lucas waited on her to pack a bag. She'd worked with her vision rehabilitation therapist to start setting up her house so she could function semi-independently, but now she was being forced from the comfort of her home to stay with Lucas.

It was unnerving in more ways than one. At his cabin, she'd be totally dependent on him, a thought that incensed her.

She didn't want to need anyone. Not now. Not ever.

"Do you need help?" Lucas asked.

Charlotte squared her shoulders and shook her head. There was no way she'd allow Lucas to paw through her underwear drawer. She didn't even want him watching her sort through it.

"Why don't you wait in the living room or check on the CSI team while I gather my things?"

An awkward moment of silence ensued, then Lucas murmured his agreement. "Call me if you need help."

She did need help, but she certainly wouldn't call him. If she wore mismatched clothing, so be it.

Then again, she'd simply pack jeans. They matched

everything. No need to pack a dozen outfits. She didn't plan on being at his place long.

She used the cane Rebecca had left and counted steps to her closet, then pulled out two pairs of jeans to pack, and another one to wear on the ride.

Heat climbed her neck as she realized she was wearing her pajamas and hadn't thought of it until now. Granted, they were modest—light blue cotton pants and a tank top—but she still felt exposed. The bandage on her shoulder where she'd been shot probably stood out in plain view, too.

It hadn't occurred to her to grab a shirt or robe when she'd been running for her life.

She pulled a flannel shirt from the hanger, then found two T-shirts and her overnight bag in the corner of the closet, and carried them to her bed and placed the clothing inside. She moved toward the dresser, silently cursing when she rammed her toe on the corner of the bed.

Remembering Rebecca's advice to stop and take a deep breath when she felt confused or disoriented, she did, then made her way to the dresser and removed two sets of underwear.

Next, the challenge of her toiletry bag. She found her toothbrush and toothpaste along with her brush. No need to take a makeup bag when she couldn't see to apply it. She hardly ever wore makeup anyway. She much preferred the natural look.

She did grab moisturizer and ponytail holders for her hair. For now, that would do.

She packed them in the outside zippered compartment of her bag, then slowly made her way to the living room.

"Ready?" Lucas asked.

No. "Yes. How much longer will the investigators be here?"

"Not too long. I'll have them lock up when they leave."

She turned and glanced across the living room as if she could see it. She could in her mind.

This place had been her sanctuary. Her first real home. She'd decorated it with love.

Would she ever feel safe here again?

LUCAS REMINDED HIMSELF that he had to keep his hands off of Charlotte.

He'd crossed the line earlier. Something he'd never done before.

The realization shook him to the core.

Charlotte lapsed into silence as he drove. Was she worried that he wouldn't behave himself?

Although…she hadn't exactly resisted his kiss. She'd seemed to enjoy it.

Don't go there.

Tonight was about making her feel safe and letting her get some much-needed rest.

His wants and needs be damned.

"Have you ever been to Hawk's Landing?" Lucas asked.

Charlotte tucked a strand of her gorgeous black hair behind one ear. "Yes, I visited Honey at the cabin she and Harrison share. She showed me the plans for the development and my house."

A smile tilted his mouth. He was glad she'd come to his family's ranch, glad she'd seen it so she could picture it in her mind.

"Your land is beautiful," she said. "I didn't go in your family's farmhouse, but I'm sure it's stunning."

Lucas chuckled. "It's homey and lived-in, not a showcase," he said. "But my mother didn't want to change anything after my sister disappeared. When my father left, she fell apart for a while. I think she believed one day he'd come back and she wanted his home to be the way he remembered it."

Charlotte wet her lips with her tongue. "Do you ever hear from him?"

Pain gnawed at Lucas, sucking at his insides. "No, nothing since he left." He didn't even know if his father was dead or alive.

"I'm sorry." She felt along the seat as if searching for his hand and he reached out and took hers. Her skin felt warm, titillating. Her touch was comforting.

They sat in silence until he pulled onto the ranch. "We just passed the gate and sign for Hawk's Landing," he said, hoping to paint a mental picture for her.

The SUV bounced along the graveled road leading past the farmhouse, then he veered to the right.

"Harrison and Honey live to the left of the main house. My place is the opposite direction, but the cabin is laid out the same."

"I know they're excited about the new house they're building," Charlotte said.

"Yeah, they wanted something bigger. I guess for when the baby comes."

Charlotte nodded, but lapsed into silence again. He wondered if she'd ever been married or come close, but refrained from asking.

Best he not go there. She might think he was pry-ing or interested, and he didn't want to give her the wrong idea.

It had never occurred to him to settle down and have a family. But these last few months, as he'd watched his older brother and Honey, he realized it would be wonderful to have someone to love you.

He spotted two horses galloping in the pasture and realized one of his brothers had added to their equine population. They'd talked about ranching again, but he didn't know how they'd manage with all their careers.

"We're here," he announced as he parked in front of the cabin. The rustic wood architecture set against the backdrop of the lush pastures brought a smile to his mouth.

This place was home. His safe haven.

He wanted it to be the same for Charlotte.

But she looked nervous as he led her into the house.

"If you'll describe the layout again, it will help," she said, her voice brittle with emotions he didn't quite understand.

"It's actually similar to your house," he said. "A wide foyer as we enter with a table for keys by the door. Open concept with the den to the right. A fireplace is on the far wall, a dark brown leather sofa facing it. The dining area is to the left of the living room with the kitchen behind it. A hallway is straight ahead and leads to two bedrooms, each with their own bath. The first one is the master and slightly bigger. If you want it, I can take the other room—"

"No, the guest room is fine." She stood ramrod-straight. "I think I'll lie down now."

"Of course." She must be exhausted. He took her

hand and led her down the hall past his room to the guest room. She stopped at the door. "Let me count so I can learn my way around."

"Sure. The bed is on the left wall by the window. There's a small dresser by the door, where we are now. The bathroom is to the right."

He guided her through the layout, giving her time to acclimate, then into the bathroom. "There are towels on the hook to your left and a cup for water on the sink. Hand soap is in the dispenser. If you need shampoo, I can bring some in from my bathroom."

"Not tonight," she said. "I showered at the hospital."

The hospital. That seemed like days ago, but was only a couple of hours.

"I can turn the bed down if you want."

"No," she said. "Please just leave me alone. I'll manage."

Her curt tone made him stiffen, but how could he blame her for being short with him after all she'd been through?

The urge to pull her in his arms again teased him, but he fought it off.

He didn't want her to worry that he'd start pawing at her again.

"Call me if you need anything, Charlotte."

She felt her way to the bed, and starting turning down the quilt. "Thank you, Lucas."

He stared at her for a long minute, soaking in her beauty and strength.

"Good night, Charlotte," he said gruffly.

"Good night, Lucas."

Having her in his house, sleeping in his guest room, seemed more intimate than he could ever imagine.

But he forced himself to give her privacy and left the room.

CHARLOTTE HADN'T THOUGHT she'd sleep, but fatigue and her surgery worked a number on her and she fell fast asleep.

The next morning, as she stretched, she realized she hadn't had nightmares. She'd felt safe in Lucas's house.

But with no word from the girls, she didn't want to get up and face the day.

Depression…she understood its call. She'd felt it before.

She had to fight its strong pull.

She rubbed her eyes and blinked, praying that a miracle had happened while she slept and her vision was restored, but no. A flash of light maybe. But then everything went dark again.

Heaving a weary sigh, she forced herself to sit up and mentally orient herself. The bathroom—which way was it?

Frustration warred with the need to talk to Lucas and see if he'd heard any news.

Courage fortified, she slid her legs to the side of the bed, retrieved her cane and mentally focused on finding her way to the bathroom. A quick wash of her face, and she remembered to throw on a shirt over her tank top, then felt her way to the door.

The cabin was quiet. But the scent of coffee wafted toward her, and she followed it to the kitchen.

She paused, unsure what to do. She kept her mugs on the counter by the coffeepot. Where did Lucas keep his?

Tears threatened, but she blinked them back. She was not going to cry over something as unimportant as a cup of coffee when her students' lives were so much more important.

She felt along the counter, hoping to find a coffee mug, but the sound of the door screeching startled her. She froze. Lucas?

"It's me," he said earning a smile of relief from her. "I went for a run earlier and showered. Just got off the phone with the deputy. He's doing well, went home last night so that's a good sign." A pause and he was walking toward her. "I didn't know if you were a coffee drinker or tea, but I'm addicted to coffee myself."

She relaxed, grateful for his attempt to provide some normalcy to her morning.

He took her hand, and she tensed, fighting the need to lean into him. Lucas certainly wasn't trying to seduce her, but she was seduced by his smell, his voice. His protective, caring touch.

LUCAS SUCKED IN a breath, mentally wrangling in his desires as he moved Charlotte's hand along the counter to the cupboard and his mugs. He could simply get her a cup, but for some reason, it was important to him that she be able to find her way in his house.

Maybe he wanted her here more often…

His phone buzzed.

Thank God. He needed work, not to be alone with Charlotte. He hadn't slept more than an hour for wanting her in his own bed.

"I need to get this. It's Keenan."

"All right."

He poured her a cup of coffee. "Cream? Sugar?"

She shook her head. "No, thanks."

He handed the cup to her, then connected the call.

"We identified the man at Ms. Reacher's house. His name is Damarus Morez. He showed up in the international database. He's wanted as a suspect in several teenage abductions in Mexico."

"What else?"

"We've linked him to a trafficking ring that may have ties in Austin."

"Any specifics?"

His phone beeped in with a text from his brother Dexter. His PI business in Austin had been a help more than once.

Been researching the sex trafficking in the city. May have a lead. An auction is happening tonight.

Lucas's pulse jumped. The idea of an auction sickened him.

But it might be just the lead they needed to catch this damn trafficking ring and find the missing girls.

EVIE WAS BARELY holding it together. She'd lost track of time. They'd been taken two days ago, or was it three or four? Time was all running together.

Her head felt fuzzy from whatever drug they'd forced into her water. So far they'd moved them to two different locations. The first one, that farm, she thought it hadn't been far from Tumbleweed. She'd scratched the words *Help us* on the wall, hoping someone would find it and hunt for them.

She and the others had been kept in the back of the van when they were driving, but there were no windows, so she couldn't see out. She'd listened for sounds of other cars or a city, maybe a bus or train station.

But the van seemed insulated from the sounds outside, and she'd been so tired from the drugs that she'd lost consciousness.

Mae Lynn had that desolate look on her face, as if she'd checked out of the world. She didn't fight or talk or ask questions like Evie did.

They were moving again. She'd heard them talking and they had something planned for later tonight. Something big.

Nerves clenched her stomach into a knot. It didn't sound good.

The van bumped over a pothole and tossed her to the side. She tried to catch herself, but her head hit the metal interior. It wasn't the first time and probably wouldn't be the last. She was bruised and banged up from their rough handling and the ride.

Tires screeched and the van swerved again. She looked over at Adrian and Agnes. They were awake, clinging to each other. Mae Lynn seemed most affected by the drugs, or maybe she just wanted to sleep so she didn't have to face what was happening.

Evie wanted to sleep, too. But she knew better. Sleeping wouldn't stop anything bad from happening. She wanted to be alert, strong, ready to fight if she got the chance.

The van suddenly slowed, gears grinding. Another bump then they turned right and screeched to a stop. Adrian looked at her, wide-eyed.

"What's happening?" Agnes whispered shakily.

Evie held her breath. Their wrists were still bound with zip ties. As much as she'd struggled and tried to break them, she couldn't. Her wrists were bloody from her efforts, a fact that had amused one of the brutes.

The back door opened. Was this one of the bath-room breaks they allowed them? So far, they'd only let them out at isolated areas, where there was nothing around them.

No place to run or hide, or way to call out for help.

She gritted her teeth as the biggest of the men, the animal who'd shot Ms. Charlotte, glared at her. His toothy grin gave her the creeps.

They'd left their masks off the last two times they'd opened the door. She knew what that meant. They wouldn't let her or the other girls live to identify them.

Adrian and Agnes shrank back as he climbed inside. He gave them an odd look then came toward her. Evie bit her tongue. She wanted to kick out at him, but she'd tried that already and gotten a double dose of drugs for it. Besides, he was over two hundred pounds, all mus-cle and ugliness.

He snatched her arm. "Come on. Time to say bye-bye to your friends."

Evie gasped as his fingers closed around her arm in a viselike grip. "Why are you separating us?" she asked.

"We have a special place for you." His nasty chuckle reverberated through the van as he dragged her to the edge.

"No, don't take her!" Adrian cried.

"Please keep us together," Agnes shouted.

He ignored them and dragged her out of the van. Her friend's screams echoed behind her as he shoved her inside the back of another black cargo van.

He slammed the door shut and she huddled in the dark corner, alone and terrified that she'd never see them or Ms. Charlotte again.

Chapter Eighteen

"I have to go to Austin, Charlotte. My brother, Dexter, thinks he may have a lead on the trafficking ring."

Hope bubbled in Charlotte's chest. "He knows where Evie and Mac Lynn and Agnes and Adrian are?"

Lucas shifted, hesitating long enough to indicate he didn't have the answer she wanted. Odd, even without her vision, she felt connected to him.

She understood the nuances of his voice and movements.

"He didn't mention them specifically."

Charlotte sighed. "Then what did he say?"

Another hesitation.

"Tell me the truth, Lucas. I may not like it, but not knowing is just as difficult.

"I can't bear to think that you'll lie to me or keep information from me."

Lucas stepped closer, captured her hand in his. "I won't lie to you," he said, his voice gruff, full of conviction. "You're too deep in this. You deserve to know the truth."

"The scenarios that keep playing in my mind are too horrible to say out loud."

"I understand. All the years my sister was missing, my family was plagued by nightmares of what might be happening to her. Finding out she was dead was terrible, but at least we could give her a proper burial and finally grieve for her."

Charlotte nodded. He did understand. "So what is the lead?"

"Dexter's a PI. He's made a lot of contacts on the streets. He's heard chatter about an auction tonight outside Austin."

Charlotte's stomach roiled. "An auction? You mean to sell the girls?"

A pained heartbeat passed. "Yes. He's trying to set us up as potential buyers."

"My God." She touched Lucas's arm. "It sounds dangerous."

"Don't worry about me. I can take care of myself."

"Please be careful."

He pressed a kiss to her hand. "I'd like to take you to the main house to stay with my mother while I'm gone."

"Lucas, I don't want to endanger your mother."

"These men have no idea you're at Hawk's Landing. Besides, the ranch hands will watch out for anyone coming onto the property."

Charlotte didn't want any of his men to get hurt protecting her. But she also didn't want to be alone again.

"Come on," he said. "You'll like my mother. And I found a kitten that I brought to the ranch. You can help her with that."

Charlotte knew he was trying to distract her from

thinking about the auction and from worrying about her students.

Nothing could keep her from thinking about them, though.

She wouldn't rest until they were found safe and sound.

LUCAS HAD NEVER taken a girl—woman—home before.

Not that Charlotte and he were in a romantic relationship. They weren't.

She was a job. A witness to a crime and he needed to protect her.

Still, it felt odd introducing her to his mother.

Harrison sent a text saying two of the ranch hands he'd recently hired would be watching the entry points to the ranch and that Brayden would watch the house.

Harrison had also instructed Honey's building crew to be on the alert for any strange men lurking near her job sites.

He doubted the kidnappers had made a connection to Honey, but they couldn't be too careful.

This trafficking ring was broadly spread and might have contacts in town or nearby.

He hated like hell to think that one of Tumbleweed's own residents would engage in sex slavery, but it was possible.

"Will you be back tonight?" Charlotte asked.

"I should be. If not, you can stay in the house with Mom."

Charlotte massaged her temple. Her stitches were healing, but she still had visible bruises and discolored skin from the attack.

Seeing the bandage where she'd been shot had done something to him, made him furious and more determined to find the bastard who hurt her.

"I hate to impose on your family," Charlotte said.

"You aren't imposing. My mother gets lonely now we all have places of our own."

"But you're close by," Charlotte said.

"True. And we all have dinner together once a week. Mom insists."

"That sounds nice," Charlotte said. "I can't imagine having a close-knit family."

"There's been tension over the years," Lucas said. "My brothers and I felt responsible for Chrissy's disappearance. We tried to make it up to Mom, but nothing can take the place of a missing or lost child."

Emotions clouded Charlotte's face, and Lucas wished he'd kept his mouth shut.

He led Charlotte to his SUV and drove the short distance to the ranch house in silence. When he parked, he came around to the passenger side and helped Charlotte from the car.

"There's a porch with five steps leading up to it."

Charlotte nodded and took his arm. The gesture made his chest squeeze. At least she was beginning to feel comfortable with him. Beginning to trust him.

He couldn't let her down.

CHARLOTTE SWALLOWED HER pride and held her head high as Lucas guided her up the steps and into his family's house.

Honey had told her a lot about the Hawks, how Mrs.

Hawk had disliked her when she was growing up, had thought she wasn't good enough for the Hawk family.

Charlotte had decided then that she detested the woman. Honey was the sweetest woman and best friend she'd ever had.

But Honey had insisted that she and Mrs. Hawk had a long talk, and had come to an understanding. That now Mrs. Hawk treated her like a daughter.

Footsteps clicked on floors that were made of wood. The scents of cinnamon and vanilla wafted to her, wind chimes from the porch tinkling as Lucas closed the front door.

"Lucas, I'm so glad you came by."

A second passed, and she felt movement, then realized Mrs. Hawk must be hugging her son.

A second later, she shook Charlotte's hand. "It's so nice to finally meet you, Charlotte. Honey and Harrison have talked about you for months."

The woman's skin was soft, her voice low, melodic. "I'm so sorry, dear, for what you've been going through."

Emotions flooded Charlotte. "Thank you. I told Lucas I don't want to stay here if it's going to put you in harm's way."

"Nonsense," Mrs. Hawk said with a light laugh. "I have four sons and trust all of them to keep us safe."

Something soft brushed against Charlotte's leg. Then she heard a tiny purring sound.

"Sandstorm likes you."

"Sandstorm?" Charlotte said.

"The kitten Lucas brought home."

Lucas brushed her arm, then placed a tiny fur ball in her arms.

Charlotte smiled and hugged the little creature. As a child, she'd always wanted a pet, but it was painful to get attached and then to be separated by a move. Her last foster parents claimed they didn't have money to feed stray animals when they had enough stray kids to care for.

"Come in the kitchen with me and let's let Lucas get going." The woman wrapped her arm around Charlotte's shoulders, and Lucas murmured that he'd be back later.

She prayed he'd return with the missing girls.

LUCAS MET DEXTER at his PI office on the edge of Austin.

As a teen, he and Harrison had worried about Dexter. He'd been rebellious and angry and made their family life hell.

The third and last time he'd skirted trouble with the law, he and Harrison had a long hard talk with him.

They hadn't bailed him out of jail. Instead, they'd let him stew for a week. Their mother had been furious at them, but Dexter had started down a road to destruction and they were desperate to steer him back on track.

When he finally got out, Dexter had been forced to do community service. Working at a teen community center for troubled boys had woken him up.

He'd balked at college and when Harrison suggested he study law enforcement, he'd resisted. Dexter didn't want to play by the rules.

He liked to make them and break them.

But at least now, he was working on the right side of the law. As long as he didn't bend the rules too far, he and his brothers kept their mouths shut.

Last year he'd even tracked down a drug lord targeting kids as young as eight.

Dexter met him at the door to his office. "Come on in and I'll fill you in."

They both grabbed coffee from the credenza in his brother's office.

"What exactly did you hear?" Lucas asked.

"Chatter about a new shipment," Dexter said. "My source said the code word for the operation is Shetland."

Lucas gritted his teeth. "Like the Shetland cattle ranch where we found a carving made by one kidnap victim."

Dexter nodded. "Word is there's an auction tonight at nine. A private select few clients will attend. All wealthy."

"All looking to buy sex slaves," Lucas said in disgust.

"Exactly." Dexter opened a closet in his office and pointed out two men's suits. Expensive. Designer.

"We have to play the part."

"You got us an invitation?" Lucas asked, impressed.

"Damn right." Dexter handed Lucas a folder. "Here's your cover story. You are—"

"Blaine Thorpe, entrepreneur and multimillionaire."

His brother had thought of everything. He just hoped the plan worked.

CHARLOTTE NIBBLED ON the most delicious cinnamon roll she'd ever tasted. Lucas hadn't mentioned that his mother was an excellent cook.

"I know you paint," Mrs. Hawk told Charlotte. "You're probably missing your art right now."

"I am," Charlotte said. "But nothing matters except finding those students."

Mrs. Hawk covered Charlotte's hand with her own. "If anyone can find them, my boys can."

The pride in the woman's voice touched Charlotte. "I know you're proud of them."

"I am. I let them down years ago when my daughter went missing, but they rallied around me and kept me strong."

"They're lucky to have you," Charlotte said and meant it.

A strained silence passed. "I wasn't always so nice to Honey," she said. "I thank God every day that she forgave me and that she's in Harrison's life. Nothing makes me happier than to know he's finally happy."

"Spoken like the best of mothers."

"Not the best, but I try." She took Charlotte's hand. "I'd like to show you something."

Charlotte stiffened. "But you know—"

"That you lost your sight temporarily? Yes."

"It might not be temporary."

"Keep the faith, Charlotte. Sometimes life gives us things we don't think we can handle, but through it we find other precious gifts."

Charlotte wanted to believe her, but worry for her students robbed her of words.

"Come on. Please."

Charlotte nodded. What else could she do?

She stood and allowed the woman to lead her into another room. A cool breeze fluttered through the window bringing the scent of fall.

"What is this room?" Charlotte said.

"It's my secret room," Mrs. Hawk said.

Charlotte wrinkled her brow.

"I haven't shown it to my sons," Mrs. Hawk continued. "It…was my therapy the last few years."

"Like my painting is for my students," Charlotte said.

"Exactly." Mrs. Hawk led her to a table and placed her hands on top of a hard mound. It felt like clay.

"Tell me what you think," Mrs. Hawk said, a sheepish note to her tone.

Charlotte hesitated, but it seemed important to the woman, so she gingerly ran her fingers over the oval shape. It was a bust.

Her heart squeezed as she traced her fingers over the heart-shaped face. A young girl's face. Pigtails. Ribbons in her hair.

"It's your daughter," Charlotte said, touched that she'd shared it with her.

"It is," Mrs. Hawk said. "This may be forward of me, but I thought since you couldn't paint right now, you might like to try the clay."

Charlotte chewed her bottom lip. She hadn't considered another art medium. And how could she possibly make something art-worthy when she couldn't see what she was doing?

"No one ever has to see it," Mrs. Hawk said as if she'd read her thoughts. "I don't show my pieces. But doing it connects me to Chrissy. And I love working with the clay."

"Are you working on something now?" Charlotte asked.

"Yes, it's a surprise for Harrison and Honey's baby. There's space at the table if you'd like to try. You don't have to make anything with it. For a long time I just pounded out my anger and frustration." She gave a self-deprecating laugh. "If you could see the walls, you'd know what I'm talking about."

Charlotte reached out her hands. "Thank you for sharing. I…might give it a try."

Mrs. Hawk guided her to another chair and a clump of clay.

Charlotte gently touched it then settled in the chair and began to pound it with her fist.

THE AUCTION WAS set to take place in the basement of a nightclub called The Silver Bullet, a trendy hot spot for young musicians and groups flocking to Austin.

Newbies wanting to be discovered started out at open-mic night at a neighboring place called the Cactus Café, then built an audience and reputation and earned bookings here.

Inside, dim lights created a bluesy feel and the walls showcased pictures of local artists who'd made it big. A corkboard at the entryway had flyers advertising upcoming acts and appearances of artists at other venues.

The band tonight, a country rock group who called themselves The Bullhorns, was in full swing.

It seemed an odd atmosphere for a sex-trafficking room, which made Lucas wonder if the owners had any idea what was going on in the space beneath them.

Lucas and Dexter made their way to the bar, fending off smiles from interested women. Truth was, Lucas didn't see anyone as attractive or interesting as Charlotte.

Dexter paused to flirt a little. Then again, that was his little brother's style.

Dexter had never met a person he couldn't talk to or charm.

Lucas leaned against the bar, waiting for Dexter to give him the signal that they could go downstairs.

His brother deftly sidled up to a dark-haired, olive-skinned man, who spoke to him in a low voice.

Dexter flicked his thumb, signaling Lucas to follow. He forced nonchalant smiles at a few of the women he passed, hoping to blend in. But he'd never been a ladies man.

The dark-haired man led them down a hallway past the restrooms, then through a sliding door that probably went unnoticed to most. It was dark inside, but the man used his phone to light the way down a stairwell to another hall with several rooms on each side.

He opened one door and gestured for them to enter.

"You both have bidding numbers at your space," the man said. "The bidding starts in five minutes."

Anger coiled in Lucas's belly, but he managed a sly grin. "Thanks."

Dexter's expression was grim as they each located their designated chairs and took seats to watch the show unfold on the computer screen.

Tension knotted every muscle in Lucas's body. He and Dexter had planned a strategy earlier.

They'd bid on the girls then call in reinforcements to make the arrests once they had the girls in sight.

It was possible the Shetland ring was holding the girls in another location. They'd secure payment, then deliver the merchandise.

He rolled his shoulders, checked his assigned number, then braced himself to play the part of an interested buyer as two men led a group of young girls across a stage.

"Promising," Dexter said beneath his breath in case the room was bugged. These men were professionals and might be monitoring the clients, looking for a possible setup.

Lucas's pulse jumped as the girls were told to look up at the camera.

It was Charlotte's students.

The sisters—Adrian and Agnes—clung to each other, both bleary-eyed with drugs. The other, Mae Lynn, stumbled, her face as pale as a ghost.

She wasn't holding up well. She looked drugged or… in shock.

He had to do something.

But one of the girls was missing. The one Charlotte called Evie.

Where the hell was she?

Chapter Nineteen

As soon as he'd learned the location of the auction, Lucas had spoken with Keenan and they'd set up a trace to search for possible phone or internet connections to the men holding the auction.

Backup was on standby, surveilling the club and surrounding area. He wanted eyes on the streets looking for a van or other vehicle that might be used to transport the kidnap victims.

A voice, smooth and polished, came over the speaker and introduced the first girl to be auctioned. He and Dexter exchanged conspiratorial looks.

This one was Adrian. A second later, the same voice relayed that her sister came with her—two for the price of one?

A bargain deal for someone wanting more excitement, or to have an extra girl to share.

The bidding began at $100,000. Dexter jumped in at $125,000. Lucas gritted his teeth and watched the girls hover together. They had been forced to change into sexy, tight outfits to accentuate the female curves still in the infancy stage.

The bidding increased, jumping back and forth from

Dexter to another man, then Dexter upped the bid by offering $250,000.

He won the bid.

"When your wire transfer is complete, we will deliver your merchandise."

It took every ounce of Lucas's effort to maintain a cool expression when he was seething inside.

Agnes cried and gripped her sister's arm as a big man in black escorted them from the stage. The camera was careful not to show the man's face.

Next the man dragged a catatonic-looking Mae Lynn onto the stage. The poor girl looked as if she'd vanished into a world of her own. Someone had made an attempt to comb her hair and apply a little makeup and lipstick, and they'd dressed her in a glittery tube top and black spandex skirt that barely covered her essentials.

She stumbled when the man released her arm and swayed on stiletto heels that made her look tall and thin.

She was obviously drugged. Her eyes were bleary and bloodshot. A wide silver bracelet dangled from her arm—it was clearly an attempt by the kidnappers to hide the bruising from the ties that had kept her prisoner.

The auctioneer spoke again, and another male voice started the bid at $50,000. Lucas waited patiently as the man who'd bid on the sisters offered a higher bid. They went back and forth for a few minutes.

When Lucas sensed they were about to end it, he jumped in with a higher bid at $150,000.

The auctioneer tried to push the bidding higher, but the other men declined. Lucas had just bought Mae Lynn.

The auctioneer assured the other two bidders that

he had more merchandise on the way and would keep them informed regarding the next auction.

Cameras inside the room prevented Lucas from checking his phone, but he hoped Keenan had traced the origin of the auctioneer.

"Transfer the money now, gentlemen," the auctioneer said. "Once we have confirmation, you'll receive word where to pick up your purchases."

The dehumanizing language the man used made Lucas's skin crawl.

But he and Dexter used their phones to complete the transactions. Keenan had arranged dummy profiles and bank accounts in advance.

Silence descended as he and Dexter waited.

Five minutes later, the transfers appeared to be complete.

"You should receive notification momentarily as to where you can collect your merchandise."

Just as the man said, a second later, a text appeared on Lucas's phone with an address.

He glanced at Dexter, who nodded, confirming that he'd received instructions as well.

They filed from the room, both feigning cool smiles as they continued to play the role.

The hallway was dimly lit, and the man who'd escorted them to the private room was following, a gun tucked into the holster inside his jacket. He escorted them out a bottom door which led to an alley.

Outside the club, it was dark. Lucas and Dexter quickly circled to the front, both alert in case they were going to be ambushed in the alley.

Patrons parked and headed to the front entrance. Loud music boomed from the speakers, the perfect cover to disguise a cry for help if one of the girls attempted to escape.

He kept his eyes trained, scanning the lot in search of the girls, but as he suspected, he didn't see them.

The men were smart. They kept the girls isolated and tucked away for safekeeping in case the auction turned into a setup.

He and Dexter got in the car and Dexter directed him to the warehouse district, where several abandoned buildings sat, desperate for renovation.

Lucas's lungs squeezed for air as he parked. Seconds later, a black van pulled up by the warehouse.

Dexter tensed, his body braced for trouble. Lucas slid one hand over his weapon. He was ready.

The van door opened and out stepped one of the kidnappers.

Another man in black, armed and muscular, slid from the passenger side, a semiautomatic in his hands.

One of their hired thugs.

The driver walked around to the back of the van and opened the door.

Lucas and Dexter eased from the car, their expressions neutral, guns hidden. They maintained the facade of the interested buyers they'd posed as.

The man with the semi aimed it at them, warning them to say stay back. Lucas held up his hands in a surrender gesture. Dexter folded his arms and leaned against the car, his look nonchalant.

Just another day of buying and selling innocent girls.

Satisfied they were compliant, the driver reached inside the van and dragged Mae Lynn from the back. Next came Adrian and Agnes.

The sisters were trembling, terrified. Mae Lynn looked completely numb.

"Thank you for doing business with us," the driver said.

He shoved the girls forward, and Lucas caught Mae Lynn before she hit the ground. Dexter swept the sisters into the back of the SUV, then grinned at the men as if to indicate he was pleased.

Lucas helped a trembling, weak-kneed Mae Lynn into the back of the SUV, too.

He leaned into the car and whispered. "FBI. We're here to help you. Stay down."

The girls looked at him wide-eyed. He gently shoved Mae Lynn's head down to her knees.

"Trust me. We're going to arrest them."

The youngest sister choked out a cry, then her sister wrapped her arm around her and pushed her head down as well.

Lucas shut the door, then turned just as the driver and man with the gun were getting inside their van.

He spoke into his mic, alerting the backup team at the club that they could move. Keenan had warrants ready.

Then he shouted at the driver. "Wait, man, there's one more thing."

The animal turned to him, suspicion flaring while the brute with the gun aimed it at Dexter.

Before the man could shoot, Dexter drew and fired at him.

Then bullets started flying.

CHARLOTTE ROLLED AND shaped and pounded the clay, uncertain what she was doing, but working with the clay relaxed her and distracted her from her current situation.

First she crafted juvenile things—a snake, a bowl, a teacup—to simply learn the feel of the clay and how to mold it in her hands.

Then she made a big ball, and tried to shape the face of the man who'd shot her.

She made a large oval shape—was his face oval? No, he had a square jaw, beefy neck, wide head... Or was that the other man?

The mask had covered their faces. Really all she'd noticed were those tattoos...

Frustrated, she rolled the clay back into one big ball again and pounded with her fists, working out her frustrations and anger.

Mrs. Hawk's footsteps, lighter than Lucas's, echoed on the wood floor. She also smelled of lavender. "You probably didn't like the first painting you did, either, did you?"

Charlotte twisted her mouth in thought. "I guess not," she admitted.

"What was the first thing you painted?"

"The ocean, but it was a dark stormy day, and it came out looking like a sea monster was rising from the waves."

"Maybe that's how you saw the world then," Mrs. Hawk said.

Charlotte smiled. Odd how she talked to her students the same way. "You're sure you aren't a therapist?" Charlotte said with a small laugh.

Mrs. Hawk rubbed her shoulder. "I spent a lot of time on the receiving side of therapy. Maybe I learned something."

"Thank you for sharing your hobby," Charlotte said.

"Only another artist could understand." She hesitated. "Although, I'm not going to tell you that I understand what it's like to lose your vision, I'll help you however I can."

"I miss seeing people's faces, their expressions. It helps me understand them."

"Body language is important. But you're probably picking up nuances in tone and people's movements now that you never noticed before."

"That's true," she said. "But I still miss the colors." Emotions welled in her throat. "I'm afraid that I'll forget what the different shades and textures look like."

"You won't," Mrs. Hawk said quietly.

Charlotte soaked in her comforting words, then ran her fingers over the clay again.

"I'd better check on dinner," Mrs. Hawk said.

"It smells heavenly," Charlotte said and meant it because it smelled like home.

"It's just my chili and jalapeno cornbread," Mrs. Hawk said. "It's simple, but all my boys love it."

Footsteps echoed again, this time going softer as the seconds passed, signaling that Lucas's mother had left the room.

An image of Lucas's handsome, strong face flashed behind her eyes. She was grateful she'd seen a picture of him before she'd lost her sight.

The day she'd run her fingers over his face had ingrained his features into her mind as well.

Taking a deep breath, she felt the clay again. This time she began to shape Lucas's face.

LUCAS'S SECOND SHOT hit the man with the semi in the abdomen while Dexter tangled with the driver.

The brute with the semi dropped to the ground, then fired at Lucas. Lucas dodged the bullet, then fired again. This time he caught the man square in the forehead. He dropped face-forward into the dirt.

The driver shoved Dexter to the ground then staggered toward the van to escape. Dexter fired at him and caught him in the back of his knee.

The man fell with a howl of pain but kept crawling to the van. Lucas rushed him and jammed his pistol into the driver's temple.

"Give me a reason to finish it," Lucas growled.

The man went still. A second later, he swung his fist out to push Lucas's gun away. The gun flew upward, a bullet was released, then pinged the side of the van.

Lucas punched the man in the jaw before he could react, then brought the butt of his weapon down and slammed it against the bastard's head.

The man's eyes rolled back in his head, and he collapsed against the steering wheel.

A siren wailed. Backup had arrived. Lucas handcuffed the man to the steering wheel, then phoned Harrison and filled him in.

"We're transporting the girls to the hospital. Bring Charlotte. They need to see her."

Chapter Twenty

Lucas explained the situation to the medics. "I'm riding with you to the hospital. I want to talk to him the minute he wakes up."

They agreed, and he went to talk to Dexter and the girls. The sisters were huddled together, terrified and wide-eyed, but obviously relieved to be rescued. Mae Lynn sat catatonic on the end of a gurney, looking pale and in shock.

"Where's Evie?" Lucas asked.

Fear darkened the sisters' eyes. "We don't know," the oldest one said. "They dragged her out of the van, put her in another one and took off."

"What about Ms. Charlotte?" the younger sister asked.

"Is she… Did she die?" the younger one asked.

Lucas wanted to soften the blow, but he wouldn't lie to the girls. "She survived and has been worried sick about you."

"We want to see her," the sister cried.

"We'll make that happen," Lucas assured them. "Although the blow to Charlotte's head caused her to experience vision loss. The doctors don't know if it's permanent or temporary." He offered them a sympathetic smile. "She's going to meet you at the hospital. Dexter will drive you."

Lucas climbed in the back of the ambulance with the unconscious driver.

He didn't intend to let the creep out of his sight.

A HALF HOUR LATER, Charlotte paced the waiting room at the hospital, waiting on the doctor to let her visit her students. Mrs. Hawk pushed a cup of coffee into her hands.

Lucas explained that one of the kidnappers was dead, and the other was in surgery. The FBI were watching the club where the auction had taken place, but were waiting to make arrests until they had information on Evie.

From Lucas's report, Mae Lynn wasn't doing well.

Charlotte brushed at tears and felt a soft hand squeeze her shoulder. Mrs. Hawk. She recognized the scent of the lavender that surrounded her.

"What will happen to them when they're released from the hospital?" Mrs. Hawk asked.

Charlotte sighed. Another worry. "I don't know. They'll probably go back into the system." Although Mae Lynn might need psychological help.

"You know I've been thinking," Mrs. Hawk said. "I mean, I haven't met these girls, and they might not be interested, but…I have a big house and a lot of empty bedrooms."

Charlotte rubbed her temple. "What are you saying?"

"I don't know what it takes to become a foster parent, but maybe the girls could stay at the ranch for a while."

Charlotte's eyes burned with tears. Although she'd feared she wouldn't like Mrs. Hawk, she and the woman had connected. And now she was offering her home to Charlotte's students. "That is awfully generous of you.

The girls would love the ranch. Adrian and Agnes are obsessed with horses. But I'll warn you. These girls had rough lives, and that was before the kidnapping. There could be deep-seated psychological trauma now."

Mrs. Hawk brushed a strand of Charlotte's hair away from her face. "Then they're lucky they'll have you to help them navigate their way."

Self-doubt plagued Charlotte. "I want to be there for them, but I'm not sure what good I can do now."

Mrs. Hawk cupped Charlotte's face in her hands. Like her touch, her voice was gentle. "You are exactly what they need, dear."

Charlotte clung to the woman's words, hoping she could live up to Mrs. Hawk's faith in her. Then she wrapped her courage around her like a cloak and prayed they'd find Evie.

LUCAS SAW THE worry on Charlotte's face and wanted to comfort her. "We're waiting on the doctors to finish their evaluation, then you can see the girls."

"How did they seem?" Charlotte asked.

"The sisters are shaken, and it was evident that they'd been drugged. Other than that, they don't appear to be physically harmed. They claimed they were not sexually assaulted."

Relief filled Charlotte's sigh. "Thank God. But you said Mae Lynn seemed more traumatized?"

He nodded. He wouldn't speculate on her condition, but she hadn't looked good.

Lucas placed a comforting hand on her arm. "What was going on with you and my mother?"

Charlotte smiled softly. "Your mother is amazing.

She offered to let the girls stay at the ranch when they're released."

Lucas gaped at her in shock. "My mother wants to be a foster parent?"

Charlotte smiled. "It was her idea. She said she had a lot of empty bedrooms."

"What did you tell her?"

"I think it's a good idea, but we'll have to go through Child and Family Services."

Lucas's heart warmed. His mother had been devastated after they'd lost Chrissy.

Taking care of these teens might be the purpose she needed in life.

A doctor appeared, his face solemn as he introduced himself. "Do any of the teens you brought in have family?"

"No," Lucas answered. "They're all foster children." He'd made calls to inform those parents that the girls had been found. They had sounded relieved, but all were reluctant to take traumatized kidnap victims back into their homes.

Charlotte extended her hand and introduced herself. "I've been working with the girls in an art-therapy program. They were at my studio when they were kidnapped. How are they?"

"I'm aware of the incident," the doctor said. "How are you doing, Ms. Reacher?"

"I'm just worried about my students," Charlotte said.

"They are traumatized and shaken, but physically okay. They were given Rohypnol, but the effects aren't permanent. I'd suggest they stay overnight for observation."

"How about the girl named Mae Lynn?" Lucas asked.

"I'm concerned about her. So far she hasn't spoken or responded to any of us. The psychologist said she needs time and patience. She also may need an in-house therapy program."

"I have to see them," Charlotte said, her voice strained.

The doctor looked to Lucas for approval, and Lucas nodded. "They witnessed Charlotte being shot. They need to see that she didn't die trying to save them."

LUCAS WAS RIGHT. Charlotte repeatedly reminded herself to be strong as the doctor escorted her to Agnes and Adrian's room.

Mae Lynn was in a private room awaiting more tests.

Nerves rippled through her as she entered the sisters' hospital room. She wished she could see their faces, their expressions.

But a second later, she realized she didn't need to.

"Ms. Charlotte!"

Agnes's voice.

Footsteps sounded as Agnes ran to her and threw her arms around her. Adrian followed, her shriek echoing through the room. The force of the two of them throwing themselves at Charlotte nearly threw her off balance. Lucas caught her, his murmur of reassurance blending with the girls' cries as their tears soaked Charlotte's blouse.

She didn't care about the dampness. She wrapped her arms around them, rocking them in her arms. "I'm so glad you're all right," Charlotte whispered into their hair.

"We were so worried about you," Adrian sobbed.

"I'm sorry you got shot," Agnes cried.

"Shh, it's all right. I'm fine, and you're going to be okay, too."

She held them until their sobs slowly subsided, then with the help of Lucas, she coaxed the girls back to bed. The girls climbed on one bed together, and Charlotte sat on the end, clutching their hands in hers.

"Now talk to me," she said. "I want to know what happened while you were gone."

EVIE FELT DIZZY AGAIN. More drugs. She could have sworn they were driving in circles. She'd heard the same sound, a train, more than once.

Why would they drive in circles? To throw her off and make her think they were farther away from Tumbleweed than they were?

And what had they done with Agnes and Adrian, and poor Mae Lynn? That girl worried her. She needed to be stronger, to fight.

Evie licked her lips, but her mouth was so dry that she could hardly swallow.

Suddenly the van came to a screeching halt. She clawed at the wall to keep from sliding to the other side and hitting her head.

Willing herself to be strong and look for the right moment to run, she stretched her legs, but they felt weak, rubbery.

The back door of the van squeaked as it was opened. She held her breath, blinking back tears. She refused to cry.

Footsteps pounded on the metal floor as the man approached. It was so dark in the van she couldn't see his face, but he was big. The biggest one with the tattoos. The one who'd shot Ms. Charlotte.

She bit back a scream as he shoved some kind of cover over her head so she couldn't see.

Then he grabbed her arm and hauled her to the back of the van. A second later, her feet hit the ground. She fell, hoping to slow him by making herself heavy and limp. That just angered him. He picked her up, threw her over his shoulder and kept walking. She beat at his back with her bound hands. "Where are you taking me?"

"Stop fighting and behave," he growled.

She choked back a response. She would never stop fighting.

Chapter Twenty-One

Charlotte hugged the sisters one more time. "Will you two be all right here tonight?"

"Now we know you're okay and we're away from those men, we will be," Agnes said.

"But we have to find Evie." Adrian sighed, guilt and fear tingeing her voice. "Evie really held it together, she held *us* together."

Charlotte's throat clogged with emotion. "She is special," she said softly. "And we will find her. Agent Hawk and Sheriff Hawk won't give up until they do."

They hugged again. "What about you?" Adrian asked. "Are you going to be okay, Ms. Charlotte?"

Charlotte sucked in a deep breath. She couldn't lie to these girls, not after what they'd been through. "My vision loss may be temporary. We're not sure. But I'm working with a vision-rehabilitation therapist to help me adjust. I...will probably have to stop art classes for a while." And redo the studio if she reopened.

"As long as we can still visit or hang out with you, that's okay," Agnes said.

Charlotte squeezed their hands. "I promise. I'm here for you. Anytime you want to talk, just call."

"What about our foster family?" Adrian asked.

"I'm not certain what will happen yet," she said. "But I may know someone else who wants to be your foster mother. If it works out, I think you'll love it."

"Who is it?" Agnes asked in an anxious tone.

"I can't say yet. We have to go through the channels, but she's interested." Charlotte stood. "Now, I want to visit Mae Lynn before they throw me out of the hospital tonight." She paused. "I'll be back tomorrow, and I'll talk to your case worker about where you go from here."

She buzzed the nurse and seconds later, Haley appeared and guided her to Mae Lynn's room.

"HE'S OUT OF recovery and stirring," the doctor told Lucas. "But he needs rest—"

"I don't give a damn what he needs," Lucas said. "The bastard is part of a human-trafficking ring that abducted those four girls from the art studio in Tumbleweed."

"That may be true, but as a physician, my job is to look out for the patient's best interest."

Lucas folded his arms. "Listen to me, one of the girls is still missing. A girl named Evie. She's thirteen years old and in the hands of men who are selling her as a sex slave. Every second we waste means she's getting farther and farther away."

In spite of the doctor's concern for his patient, anger flashed in his eyes. "All right, you can go in."

Lucas thanked him, then stepped into the room and closed the door. The man was on his back, an IV hooked to him, as well as a heart monitor and oxygen tube.

Lucas crossed the room to the bed, and studied the monster who'd terrified Charlotte's students. Knowing the IV fed the man painkillers, Lucas barely restrained himself from yanking it from his arm.

Instead, he inhaled sharply then nudged his shoulder. "Wake up and talk to me, you bastard."

The man moaned, then opened his eyes and blinked, obviously disoriented.

Lucas cleared his throat. "You're in the hospital, and you're going to prison for a long time. If you want any kind of deal, you need to talk."

Confusion clouded the man's face, then awareness as he sorted through Lucas's words.

Lucas placed his fingers on the man's arm in a vise-like grip. "Where is the other girl, the one named Evie?"

The man's eyes flickered with unease, then he shook his head. "Don't know."

Anger hardened Lucas's heart. "One of your partners is dead. Who's calling the shots and what did they do with Evie?"

"Don't know," he mumbled again.

Lucas pressed his hand on the man's knee where he'd been shot and applied pressure until his eyes bulged in pain.

"I'm going to ask you one more time. Who is the leader and where is Evie?"

The man's jaw tightened. "I told you I don't know. We operate anonymously."

Lucas kept his hand on the man's knee, hinting that he would inflict more pain if he didn't talk. "How do you make connections and get your orders?"

"Burner phones. Texts. We get an address where to make a hit, then grab the Shetlands. Then we get word where to deliver the merchandise."

Rage turned Lucas's blood hot. "These are young

girls, not Shetlands or merchandise, you sick SOB. Where did they take Evie?"

The man's eyes widened as Lucas applied more pressure. "I told you I don't know," he said between clenched teeth.

"What *do* you know?" Lucas growled.

The man moaned again, his eyes rolling back in his head as if he was going to pass out. "Someone in Tumbleweed gave the orders. He wanted the last girl for himself."

Lucas went still. "Someone in Tumbleweed?"

The man nodded. "He paid in advance."

Lucas was seething. "Where were you supposed to deliver her?"

"One of the other operatives took the message. He took her while we handled transporting the other three to the auction."

Lucas applied more pressure to the man's knee, but he moaned and wailed that he didn't know anything else.

The doctor burst through the door, eyes livid. "Agent Hawk—"

Lucas threw up his hands. "He's all yours, Doc."

Pulse hammering, he strode from the room to tell Harrison. They'd search every house or business in Tumbleweed if they had to.

"Is she awake?" Charlotte asked Haley as they paused at the door.

"Not at the moment. But you can sit with her if you want. They say patients, even comatose ones, can hear when people talk to them."

Charlotte licked her dry lips. "She's always seemed

more fragile than the others," Charlotte said. "Her father abused her physically and mentally. She was just starting to open up to me."

"She'll come back to you," Haley said with confidence. "As a matter of fact, you may be just what she needs. Seeing you get shot was traumatic."

Charlotte grasped her courage. She had to assure Mae Lynn she was fine, that she didn't need to worry about her.

Haley patted her hand as she coaxed Charlotte into a chair. "You're sitting beside her bed, on her left side. There's an IV in her right arm. She was dehydrated, so we're giving her fluids."

Charlotte reached out to find Mae Lynn's hand, and Haley helped her by placing it over Mae Lynn's. "I'll leave you alone for a few minutes." Haley pushed the nurse-call button into Charlotte's lap. "Call me if you need anything."

"Thanks." She waited until she heard the door close, then she cradled Mae Lynn's hand in between hers and pressed a kiss to her palm.

Mae Lynn's breath hitched, then turned choppy.

"I'm here, Mae Lynn. It's Ms. Charlotte. You and Agnes and Adrian are safe. You're not with those men anymore. You're at the hospital in Tumbleweed."

Mae Lynn didn't respond.

"I know you were scared, and that those men treated your terribly, but you're going to be okay. You're stronger than you think, sweetie." She stroked the girl's hand repeatedly. "I'm here, and I won't leave you. I'll be with you every step of the way."

She continued to stroke Mae Lynn's hand and talk to her, relaying stories about when the girls had first met in her class to the art projects they'd worked on individually and together.

"You have real talent, Mae Lynn," Charlotte said softly. "You're strong inside. If you need to rest, that's fine, rest. But remember that you are loved. I love you and so do Agnes and Adrian and Evie."

A strangled sound echoed from the bed.

Charlotte tensed, then squeezed Mae Lynn's hand. "I'm here, honey. I'm right by your side."

"Ms. Charlotte?"

Mae Lynn's voice was weak, raw with pain.

"Yes, honey, I'm here."

Mae Lynn squeezed her hand in return, and relief flooded Charlotte.

"I thought you were dead," Mae Lynn whispered.

"No, sweetie, no way was I going to give up and leave you girls." She leaned over the bed then drew the girl into a hug. "You've been through a bad ordeal, but I promise that we're all going to get past this, Mae Lynn. We can't let those men destroy who we are."

IT WAS NEARLY midnight by the time Lucas drove Charlotte back to his house.

He left a guard to watch the man he'd shot, and he'd asked Keenan to look for possible connections to Tumbleweed.

The fact that Herman Stanley had been in Austin on business the same week the auction was held might be coincidental. Lucas didn't like coincidences.

Harrison was stopping by the banker's house to see if he'd returned, and look for anything suspicious.

Stanley's house was slightly remote. Would he bring

Evie to his house, though? That seemed chancy. How the hell would he hide her?

Although there were cases where kidnappers had held women or girls hostage practically in plain sight.

Keenan was researching Stanley's financials and assets, looking for property where he might take Evie.

A nasty taste settled in his mouth at the thought.

Charlotte remained quiet on the drive home. She looked exhausted and worried. He'd give anything to have been able to bring Evie back with the others.

He scanned the property as he drove onto the ranch, then veered down the drive to his cabin. His mother had mentioned that she'd made dinner, but he was too tired to stop by the house. Charlotte said she had no appetite anyway, and had wanted to go back to the cabin and rest.

The wind whistled through the window as he parked, and he climbed out then guided Charlotte to the cabin.

She stumbled on the top step, and mumbled an apology.

"You don't have to apologize, Charlotte. You're doing great."

A long sigh escaped her as they entered. "I don't know if I can be enough for the girls," she said, the self-doubt in her tone eating at him. "Mae Lynn is having a difficult time."

"You are strong and loving and patient. That's what they need." He brushed hair from her cheek as they entered.

"They need us to find Evie," Charlotte said. "They feel guilty that she was separated. They said that she held them together."

Lucas understood that kind of guilt. He and his

brothers had lived with it when Chrissy disappeared. "We'll find her. I promise." But would it be soon enough?

What if the man who'd bought her already had her in his clutches?

Chapter Twenty-Two

Charlotte breathed in the masculine scent of Lucas's cabin as she seated herself on his sofa. His woodsy aftershave permeated the space, reminding her that he was not only an FBI agent, but also a tough cowboy.

Emotions welled in her chest, and tears burned the backs of her eyelids. She blinked them back but failed and felt them trickling down her cheeks.

"Can I get you something to drink or do you just want to go to bed?" Lucas asked.

"Maybe a drink. I don't know if I can sleep yet."

"Wine? Beer? Whiskey? Tea?"

"Do you have red wine?"

"As a matter of fact, I do. We had some left from Harrison's wedding, so I brought a couple of bottles to the house."

She nodded, an image of sweet Evie taunting her. A minute later, Lucas tucked a wineglass into her hands. She wrapped her fingers around the glass then sniffed.

"It's a cab," she said. "My favorite."

"Good." The sound of ice clinking in a glass echoed from somewhere near the kitchen, then footsteps, and Lucas sank onto the sofa beside her.

"You're having bourbon," she said with a small smile as she recognized the strong scent.

"My drink of choice," he murmured.

They sat in silence for a moment, the tension thickening. She had the sudden urge to lean into him, to ask him to hold her. The emotions of the night bombarded her, her fear for Evie blending with worry over Mae Lynn's recovery.

"I'd better go lie down," she said, afraid she was going to fall apart.

Lucas guided her to the guest bedroom, then once again described the layout. She sipped the wine and felt for the bed.

"Call me if you need anything," he said softly.

She needed him. But she couldn't ask…

His footsteps faded and the door squeaked as he closed it. She stared into her dark world, aching to see the colors in the room, to be independent again.

But that was selfish. Evie had bigger problems and so did Mae Lynn.

Still, the day's events overwhelmed her and tears began to fall. She took another sip of wine, then felt for the end table and eased the glass onto it.

She raked her hand across the bed and found her overnight bag, then located her tank top and pajama pants. She quickly changed into them, her fingers gliding over the wound on her shoulder as she straightened her tank. She no longer needed the bandage, but she would probably have a scar.

That would be nothing compared to what the girls had to overcome.

She choked back a sob, but failed again, and the tears began to flow. The door squeaked.

"Charlotte?"

"I'm fine," she said in a raw whisper.

Footsteps echoed on the floor then his hand brushed the hair from her cheek. She swiped at the tears to no avail. They ran down her face like a river.

The bed dipped as Lucas lowered himself beside her, then he pulled her into his arms.

Charlotte didn't want to lean on him or need him. But she did need him, at least tonight.

LUCAS HELD CHARLOTTE, wanting to soothe her anxiety, but the moment she leaned into him and traced her finger over his cheek, it turned into more.

He cradled her face between his hands and closed his mouth over her lips. Her sweetness and strength triggered every protective instinct in him and aroused him at the same time.

She lifted her hand and he expected her to push him away. Instead, she raked her fingers along his jaw again, an intimate gesture that made his sex harden.

He deepened the kiss, then threaded one hand through her hair and slid the other down her back, drawing her closer.

He wanted more. Wanted all of her.

The thought sent a bolt of fear through him.

But she teased his lips apart with her tongue, and fear vanished, hunger stirring in its wake. He thrust his tongue in her mouth and stroked her back, lust driving his fingers lower, to her waist.

She felt delicate and feminine and so damn sexy that he lowered his head and trailed kisses along her neck. She lifted her head in surrender, offering him full rein. He took it, and nibbled and suckled at her throat, dipping lower and lower until he tasted the sweet saltiness of her skin above her breasts.

Her nipples stiffened to peaks beneath that thin tank top, driving him mad. His finger brushed her nipple, and she breathed in deeply.

"Charlotte, I don't want to take advantage of you," he murmured against her ear.

"You aren't." She kissed him again. "I don't want you to do this because you feel sorry for me."

That was the last thought on his mind. He moved her hand over his sex so she could feel the evidence of his desire. "That is not pity."

Her soft laugh emboldened him, and he kissed her deeper, then trailed kisses down her throat to her cleavage. He massaged one breast with his hand while he teased the other with his teeth.

She moaned softly, and tugged at his shirt. He slipped her tank top over her head, careful not to hurt her wound. It was healing, but the sight of it intensified his rage at the man who'd shot her.

"Lucas?"

"I don't want to hurt you," he whispered as he gently kissed her shoulder.

She pushed at his shirt. "You won't. It feels wonderful."

Smiling at the catch in her breath, he helped her remove his shirt, then she tugged at his belt. He'd left his gun and holster in the living room, and made quick work of shedding the rest of his clothes.

Anxious to feel her skin against his, he eased her back onto the bed and kissed her again, then looked his fill at her plump breasts. She had perfect round globes, heavy and beautiful, with rosy nipples that stood erect as if begging for his mouth.

He complied and suckled the tip of one, then drew it into his mouth. She moaned and pulled at him, stroking his back, as he eased on top of her.

She parted her thighs, then pushed at his boxers until his sex was free, hard and throbbing in her hand.

CHARLOTTE'S BODY HUMMED with desire. She'd never felt anything like the magic Lucas stirred inside her.

His fingers stroked and loved her, his mouth and lips turned her to putty in his hands.

She felt wild with need and raw with hunger.

He teased her nipples until they throbbed and ached for more. Sensations shot through her core as his fingers dipped to her femininity and he rubbed her through the thin fabric of her pajama bottoms.

She stroked his thick length, urging him toward her, and he pushed her pajamas down her legs then slipped them off. His boxers hit the floor next, then their movements became frenzied and...desperate.

She'd never wanted a man like she wanted Lucas.

She wished she could see his face, see his eyes, know that he wanted her with the same intensity.

"Don't think," he said with a tender kiss to her lips. "You can feel how much I want you, Charlotte. But if you want me to stop, I will."

"No, I want you, too." She wrapped her fingers around his erection, parted her thighs and guided him to her.

He paused a second, and she heard his jeans rustling, then realized he'd grabbed a condom. She wanted to help him but she stroked his bare hips instead, feeling the muscles of his hips flex and harden as he climbed on top of her.

He nuzzled her neck, then her breasts again, then stroked her damp center with the tip of his sex. She groaned, wanting him deeper. All the way inside her, filling her.

"You are so beautiful," he murmured.

She started to shake her head. She'd had a port-wine birthmark when she was younger, had an ugly wound now from being shot. She was…blind.

"Yes, you are," he murmured again. Without giving her time to protest, he slid his thick length inside her. She moaned, parting her legs wider to cradle his body between her thighs, then lifted her hips, inviting him deeper.

He pulled out, teased her wet center, then plunged inside her again, this time driving himself to her core. She clawed at his back, urging him to move faster and faster. Passion built a frantic rhythm, and titillating sensations spiraled through her.

Stars swam behind her eyes, and she felt dizzy, exhilarated. Deeper, deeper, harder, faster, he made love to her. She wrapped her legs around him and clung to his back as he rode her. A million delicious sensations fluttered through her, and she groaned his name as her release splintered through her.

For a moment, a sea of colors burst into a fireworks show behind her eyes. She felt dizzy. Disoriented.

Wonderful.

Tears pricked her eyes as he kissed her again, then he plunged deeper again, growling her name as his release claimed him.

LUCAS CRADLED CHARLOTTE against him. His body tingled with erotic sensations. His heart fluttered with emotions.

Charlotte nestled closer into his arms, her breathing a soft whisper against his chest.

A smile curved his mouth. She trusted him enough that she'd fallen asleep.

He'd had sex with plenty of women, but he'd never actually spent all night in a woman's bed. Never slept with one.

He started to climb from bed, but leaving her felt wrong. He wanted to hold Charlotte all night.

He wanted to listen to her breathe and feel her warm body against his. Wanted to make sure she rested and wasn't plagued by nightmares.

He wanted to love her again.

His pulse jumped.

He understood how Harrison had felt with Honey.

Being in bed with Charlotte felt right, as if they belonged together.

Fear mingled with panic. But he looked down at her and brushed her hair from her cheek. Dim moonlight played off her features, accentuating her beautiful heart-shaped face. Long dark eyelashes fluttered over her cheeks, her hair a waterfall of black against the white pillowcase.

He couldn't resist. He dropped another kiss into her hair, then another one on her cheek. She made a low murmur of contentment and snuggled deeper into his arms, and he held her tight.

He was in love with Charlotte.

But he didn't know what the hell to do about it.

She'd worried he was making love to her out of pity.

What would she think if he confessed that he was in love with her?

It was rotten timing. She had a boatload of problems. He had a job to finish.

She might misread his motives.

He kissed her forehead and closed his eyes, savoring the feel of her in his arms, and decided to wait.

He might feel differently tomorrow.

No, you won't. You fell in love with her the moment you met her.

But what if she didn't love him back?

CHARLOTTE STIRRED THE next morning, feeling sore but languid and safe in Lucas's arms.

She hadn't contemplated the consequences of making love to Lucas the night before. She hadn't thought of anything but being close to him.

The morning after was always awkward. Or it should have been.

But Lucas surprised her by kissing her good-morning, then bringing her coffee in bed.

Self-conscious, she tugged the covers over her. She probably had bed head and needed a shower.

"You look beautiful," he said.

She blushed and sipped her coffee. "We have to do something today to get Evie back."

"Charlotte," Lucas said softly. "We have feelers searching for connections to Stanley and any place he might have taken Evie."

"That's not enough," Charlotte said. Stanley might not even be involved. "I want you to call that reporter and set up a live interview."

"I don't think that's a good idea," Lucas said.

"I understand you want to keep me safe," she said. "And I appreciate it. But if I go on camera and make a plea for help, someone who knows about this trafficking ring might hear the message and call in."

Lucas's footsteps pounded across the floor. "No."

Charlotte squared her shoulders. "It's not up to you, Lucas. If you don't set it up, I'll get Harrison or someone else to help me."

He stalked from the room, and Charlotte felt for the table, put her coffee cup on it, then found her overnight bag and fresh clothes. She felt her way to the bathroom and quickly showered.

By the time she came out of the bathroom, voices echoed in the living room. Lucas's and Harrison's.

"I am not going to stand by and watch her make a target of herself," Lucas said.

"We'll be there to protect her," Harrison said.

"No, she might get hurt."

"Listen, brother, we're doing everything possible to find out who bought Evie, but time is of the essence. This creep may be taking her someplace where we'll never find her."

Charlotte's insides chilled. Harrison spoke the truth. She knew it and so did Lucas.

She struggled to recall the layout of the bedroom, then felt along the wall until she reached the door. It was partially open, so she stepped into the entryway, her chin lifted high.

"He's right, Lucas. Either call the reporter and set it up, or Harrison and I will arrange it without you."

Chapter Twenty-Three

An hour later, Lucas watched Charlotte speak into the camera, his stomach in knots. Even if he understood her need to go public, he didn't like putting her in the spotlight.

The leader of this trafficking ring might send someone after her again—or come after her himself.

On the way to the station, she'd suggested that would be a good thing. He would be close by, catch this bastard and end this nightmare by bringing Evie home.

But it was damn dangerous. A million things could go wrong.

Gerald Ingram, the blasted reporter who'd leaked the story that Charlotte had survived had been reprimanded by his boss. Lucas intentionally asked for someone else to run this interview, hoping to make a point with the creep.

The SOB Lucas had shot and taken to the hospital was on the mend and now in custody. But he still hadn't offered any more information.

"Thank God and thank the FBI and Sheriff Harrison Hawk for working diligently to stop this human-trafficking room. They have made one arrest and rescued three of the students who were taken from my studio." Charlotte paused and cleared her throat, her emotions brimming on the surface. "But one girl, thirteen-year-old Evie Cranton, is still missing." A photo of Evie appeared on the screen. "Evie is sweet and likes to paint sunsets and flowers. She's just an innocent teenager caught in a horrible situation." She paused again, this time for effect to give viewers time to make a personal connection to Evie. "Think about it, folks. This trafficking ring kidnaps young girls and sells them as sex slaves. It could be your daughter or granddaughter or your little sister or your friend who's taken next."

Lucas couldn't help but think about Chrissy and all the parents with missing kids who still had no clue where their child was. The pain was unbearable; it ate at you every day.

"The police believe that someone in our very town of Tumbleweed may be involved in this trafficking ring," Charlotte continued. "If you know anything about the men who abducted the students from Tumbleweed, please call the FBI or your local law enforcement. Let's stop this inhumane practice of stealing children and women and turning them into sex slaves, and make our town safe again."

Lucas and Harrison exchanged looks as the news anchor recited phone numbers for the Bureau and the sheriff's office.

Lucas moved quickly to extricate Charlotte from Ingram, who'd shown up at the interview like a vulture stalking his prey. The minute they'd arrived, he'd accosted her with a dozen questions about her condition and the health of the three girls they'd rescued. Lucas had threatened him with an harassment charge and steered Charlotte to Ingram's competitor.

"Just tell us—"

"That's enough." Lucas shoved Ingram away with a feral look. "Leave her alone." He quickly ushered Charlotte into the hall away from the creep.

"You did great, Charlotte," Lucas said, the pride in his voice sincere.

"I just hope it works and someone calls in. Evie was strong when she was with the other girls, but on her own, she may crumble."

Lucas escorted her to the elevator, then out the front door. They'd already set up a plan. He would leave her on the sidewalk to retrieve the SUV, but Harrison was watching. They'd also attached a wire inside Charlotte's shirt just in case something went wrong and someone from Shetland tried to grab her.

"Stay on the curb," Lucas said, close to her ear. "I'll get the car."

Car horns blared from the morning traffic, pedestrians' chatter and footsteps adding to the noise.

Charlotte worried her bottom lip with her teeth. "I'm not about to try to cross the street yet."

Her comment reminded him of her limitations and the challenges she faced.

He didn't care. He would be there to help her if she let him.

CHARLOTTE CLENCHED HER hands by her side, silently reassuring herself that she was safe. Lucas and Harrison were professionals. If something went wrong, she was wearing a wire so they could trace her.

She took a deep breath for courage. She just hoped

her TV plea did some good. Hopefully someone in Tumbleweed would see sweet Evie's picture and come forward with information to help them.

If not, and someone from the group targeted her again, she'd try to get them to talk and reveal where they'd taken Evie.

She'd do anything to save that girl.

Wind whooshed as cars raced by. Brakes squealed. Someone shouted behind her. A horn honked. Birds twittered from the tops of the trees close by. A semi-truck roared past. Loud music blared from another car.

The town was alive and bustling with noise and people. Someone brushed her side as they passed. She stumbled and clawed for balance.

Tires screeched again. Another horn. Then another push. This time someone touched her back. Not gently either—they gave her a shove.

The sound of car breaks squealing rent the air. Then hard fingers closed around her arm and she pitched forward. Another shove and she tried to scream.

A hand covered her mouth and a pungent odor clogged her nose. Her eyes burned and she gagged, choking for air.

Then the world tilted and spun, and she fell into the darkness.

PANIC SHOT THROUGH Lucas as he rounded the corner with the SUV and spotted a man in black drag Charlotte into the back of a van.

Harrison darted from the overhang of the building at a dead run and tried to stop what was happening. But the men were too quick, and the van sped off.

They had discussed this scenario, but talking about it

hadn't prepared him for the visceral fear that engulfed him at seeing Charlotte in the hands of these monsters.

What if they killed her before he could save her?

He braked and slowed just enough for Harrison to jump in the passenger side. His jaw was tight, his eyes focused on the van as it swerved through traffic.

Lucas sped up, weaving between cars to follow. He'd outfitted the SUV with a siren and he flipped it on.

He could not lose Charlotte.

"They're taking a right up there," Harrison said.

"Got it." Lucas slammed on his horn and maneuvered around a fender bender clogging traffic. By the time he made it to the turn, the van had disappeared.

He pressed the accelerator to the floor, determined not to lose the van as it roared down a side road and sped into the wilderness.

Just as he rounded a corner, a white van pulled out. He swerved to avoid hitting it. A gunshot blasted the side of his SUV, and he cursed and spun the SUV around.

Harrison ducked to avoid being hit and the passenger window exploded, glass spraying. His brother pulled his gun, leaned out the window and fired at the van.

The van backed up, then a shooter fired back as the van roared straight toward them. Lucas jerked the SUV to the right but the van slammed into his side and sent him into a spin.

Cursing, he tried to regain control, but the SUV rammed into a boulder, the front crunching as the vehicle screeched to a stop. He and Harrison acted on instinct, threw their car doors open and jumped out, taking cover behind the doors.

He fired at the van and Harrison did the same. He hit

the windshield and Harrison aimed for the tires, but a spray of bullets forced them to take cover again. Then the van's engine roared, the driver backed up and spun in the opposite direction.

Lucas darted from behind the door and fired at the tires, desperate to stop them from escaping, but dust and gravel spewed behind the van and it raced away.

He and Harrison chased after it, repeatedly firing, but a cloud of dust swirled in a blinding fog as it disappeared.

"Dammit," Lucas said. "That was a setup."

"They figured we'd be watching her," Harrison agreed.

Panic ripped at Lucas. "We can't lose her, Harrison."

Harrison wiped dust and sweat from his forehead. "We won't. She's wired."

Lucas nodded, although these guys were professionals. If they'd expected her interview was a setup, they might also anticipate a wire.

He punched Keenan's number. If they found that wire and destroyed it, they'd lose contact with Charlotte.

Then they might never find her.

CHARLOTTE STIRRED, her head throbbing. She blinked, trying to orient herself, but the darkness consumed her.

They were moving. Traffic noises outside echoed loudly. A horn honking. She was thrown sideways and pain ricocheted through her shoulders as she hit the wall of the vehicle. A van.

Was this the same one the men had used to carry Evie in?

Tears of panic and terror burned her eyes. Where was

poor little Evie? Had they already sold her and forced her to have sex with the sick man who'd purchased her?

The van careened to the right and she clawed at the floor to keep from sliding, but lost her grip and slammed against the other side.

Fighting panic, she tried to make a mental plan. They hadn't bound her hands or feet, so when they finally stopped she could try to escape.

But…how could she run when she couldn't see where she was headed?

Frustration mingled with fear, but she choked it back. Lucas and Harrison were watching. They had probably followed the van.

When her abductors stopped, they would storm the men and force them to tell them where Evie was being held.

Grasping on to hope, she blinked back tears. The Hawk brothers would save her. Then they'd rescue Evie and bring her back home, and she and the other girls would be reunited.

Tries squealed and the van suddenly lurched to a stop. She hit the side of the interior again, and gritted her teeth to keep from screaming as the back door of the van screeched open.

A faint stream of light filtered through the darkness, and pain splintered Charlotte's temple. She rubbed her forehead, but the light flickered then faded just as a hard, cold hand jerked her arm.

"What are we going to do with her?"

"Check her for a wire," a second man ordered.

Charlotte bit back a cry as they dragged her from the back. One of them ripped at her shirt. She tried to

fight, but he shoved her up against something rough—
a tree, she realized.

Then he tore the wire from inside her shirt and
pressed the tip of his gun to her head.

Lucas had never been so terrified in his life. They'd
lost Charlotte.

"They just stopped," Keenan told him over the phone.
"The signal is there, but they're no longer moving."

"Send me the coordinates."

"On the way."

A second later, he received the text and turned to
Harrison. While he'd called Keenan, Harrison had
worked on the SUV to make sure it was drivable.

"It's a little rough," Harrison said, noting the broken
window and dents in the front.

"Doesn't matter. We don't have time to wait on another vehicle. Keenan says they've stopped." Which
could mean anything.

They were transferring vehicles. Leaving Charlotte
at a specified location.

Or…

No…he couldn't let his mind go there.

"I'm checking out a couple of leads that came in on
that tip line," Keenan said. "Maybe Charlotte's interview did some good and prompted someone to come
forward."

He hoped so, but more often than not, going public
triggered countless crank calls, false leads, even false
confessions from attention seekers.

He tossed Harrison the keys. "You drive. Keenan is
checking out a couple of leads."

Harrison caught the keys in one hand then slid into

the driver's seat. Lucas jumped in the passenger side and buckled up as Harrison sped onto the road.

He gave Harrison directions, and they raced down a side road that seemed to lead nowhere. Rough terrain, then more ranches and farmland spread before them. The mountains stood in the far distance.

It seemed like forever but finally Harrison veered onto a dirt road that disappeared into a wooded section.

Lucas's pulse raced. This remote location wasn't a good sign.

He scanned the area as Harrison came to an abrupt stop. "This is it."

His brother's concerned expression mirrored the fear clawing at Lucas.

Lucas scoped out the area in search of a house or cabin, but there were no buildings in sight.

He and Harrison opened their doors with caution, prepared for another ambush. The trees rustled in the wind as leaves rained down.

His gun at the ready, Lucas glanced into the woods in search of a shooter, but everything seemed quiet.

"There are tire marks," Harrison said, pointing to the ground. "They stopped here, then it looks like they turned around and left again."

"But this is where Keenan traced the wire."

A dark foreboding swept over Lucas.

Either the kidnappers had stopped here and stripped off the wire or…they'd killed Charlotte and dumped her body in the woods.

Chapter Twenty-Four

"We have to make sure she's not here," Lucas said, his throat thick with fear.

Harrison nodded grimly, then they both began to comb the area. Weeds and trees so thick and close together they almost touched made it difficult to see, but in the next hour they searched every inch of space within a mile radius.

Sweat dampened Lucas's forehead, and he swiped at it with his sleeve, relieved that he hadn't found Charlotte's body. If she was still alive, they had a chance to save her.

He *had* to save her. She meant more to him than any woman ever had or ever would.

His phone buzzed on his hip. He quickly checked it and connected. "Keenan, they found Charlotte's wire and dumped it here, but we haven't found her. Please tell me you have something."

"I'm not sure but it's an address you should check out. It came in on an anonymous tip."

"What is it?"

"A ranch about thirty miles from where you are now."

"Do you know who sent you the tip?"

"No, but I'm trying to trace the IP address. I'll keep you posted. I'm sending you the coordinates now."

They ended the call, then Lucas motioned to Harrison to get back in the car. By the time his brother had started the SUV, the directions came through. He relayed the information to Harrison, and a frown marred his face.

"I know where that is," Harrison said as he reached for his phone. "It's another property that Stanley took over when Wilson Channing died."

"That might mean that Stanley is involved."

Harrison nodded, then tossed Lucas his phone. "Call the deputy and tell him I said to pick up Stanley. If he knows something, he's going to tell us this time."

Lucas made the call while Harrison sped onto what appeared to be a deserted road. Scrub brush and cacti dotted the landscape, with an occasional abandoned or run-down house along the way.

Lucas's heart hammered as they finally neared the ranch. Harrison slowed, and they assessed the property from a distance.

Lucas used binoculars to get a better look. "I see a Mercedes and a BMW and a dark van."

"Someone's there then," Harrison said. "Do you see any of the kidnappers?"

Lucas sucked in a sharp breath. "Actually, one just got out of the van. God…he has Charlotte."

Harrison pulled the SUV into the woods between a clump of trees. "She look okay?"

"She's alive," he said when she beat at the man's back with her fists.

He removed his weapon from his holster, retrieved

extra ammunition from the glove compartment and reloaded his gun. "Let's go get her."

Harrison checked his own weapon, and they eased from the SUV. They crept through the edge of the woods, senses alert in case the men had surveillance cameras on the premises or someone stationed as a guard.

They inched their way up to the big two-story farmhouse. Three guest cabins were situated on the property. The bastards could be using the cabins as a brothel.

Disgust turned his stomach. Harrison motioned that he would cause a distraction to draw out one or more of the men. They had no idea how many were inside, so Lucas nodded agreement and gestured that he'd go around back and look inside.

Harrison picked up a rock from the ground and threw it toward the van parked by the house. It pinged off the metal, then he threw another one.

Seconds later, two armed men stormed outside. Harrison raised his gun and shouted. "Drop it. You're under arrest."

The men whirled on Harrison and opened fire, and Harrison shot back. Lucas raced around to the back of the house and inched to the door. He peeked through the back window into a large kitchen, which was set up with a bar and plenty of booze.

Shots echoed from the front, and he prayed Harrison was safe as he crept into the house.

A big man with tattoos just like Charlotte had described raced down the steps in killer mode, his gun at the ready.

Lucas aimed his gun. "Move and I'll shoot."

The bastard whipped around and fired at Lucas. He released a shot, nailing the brute in the forehead. His eyes widened for a fraction of a second, then the big lug tumbled headfirst down the steps and collapsed on the wood floor at the bottom.

A scream echoed from above, and Lucas grabbed the man's gun and carried it with him as he raced up the steps. Behind him, the front door swung open.

He pivoted, gun aimed, ready to kill the other men, but Harrison stood in the entrance. "They're down."

Lucas gestured to the man on the floor then pointed up the steps. Harrison followed on his tail as Lucas climbed the steps. A cry sounded from the right, and he veered toward it.

Harrison went left to check the other rooms, and Lucas inched toward the rooms on the right. He peered inside one, and his stomach revolted. Two teenage girls were tied to beds, both drugged and out of it.

Not Evie or Charlotte, though. He would come back for these girls.

He inched toward the next room and heard a sob. Then Charlotte's voice. "Shh, Evie, it'll be all right."

Relief surged through him, and he pushed open the door. Another man stood with a gun aimed at Charlotte and Evie. He glared at Lucas, a warning that he'd shoot them if Lucas made a move.

Lucas didn't hesitate. He put a bullet between the man's eyes. Evie screamed and Charlotte hugged the girl to her and rocked her as Lucas stalked toward them.

"It's me, Charlotte," Lucas said. "The men are all dead."

Charlotte was trembling, soothing Evie, and he dropped to his knees and pulled them both against him.

Her tears came in a rush, and he held her tight. He didn't know what he would have done if he'd been too late and he'd lost her.

CHARLOTTE COULDN'T CONTAIN her emotions. She'd lived in fear the past few days, but the nightmare was finally over and Evie was safe.

She hugged the girl and Lucas at the same time, grateful they were all alive.

When she'd heard the gunfire, she'd been terrified that he'd been killed trying to save her.

He rubbed her back and pressed kisses in her hair. "Are you okay, Charlotte?"

She nodded against him. "I was terrified you'd been shot."

"No, I'm good." He lifted his head. "Evie, are you all right?"

"I am now," the girl said, her voice filled with anger. "What about the others?"

"They're at the hospital, but they're fine," Charlotte assured her.

Footsteps sounded, then Harrison's voice. "I've called for a couple of ambulances and CSI. There are four other girls here."

Lucas helped Charlotte and Evie stand. "Let's go outside and wait for the medics."

"Bronson called," Harrison said. "He just brought Stanley in. Said the man confessed that he knew about the trafficking ring. He's the one who called in the tip. He wants a deal for helping us."

Lucas tensed. "That depends on what else he can tell us."

He ushered Charlotte and Evie down the stairs. Evie winced when she saw the dead man, then stopped and kicked the bastard.

Sirens wailed outside, announcing the arrival of the medics and crime team. Harrison met one of the ambulances and escorted the medics upstairs to evaluate the other girls and arrange for them to be transported to the hospital for evaluation, and then for their families or foster families to be notified.

"I want to see Adrian and Agnes and Mae Lynn," Evie said in a pained whisper.

"We'll take you there," Lucas assured her.

He asked the medics to check out Evie and Charlotte while he went to help Harrison untie the other four girls.

Two HOURS LATER, after making certain Charlotte and Evie were examined and reunited with Charlotte's other students, and the four hostages they'd rescued were safe and being treated for trauma and drugs in their system, Lucas and Harrison drove to the sheriff's office to speak with Stanley.

The banker was a creep in the worst way. Not only had he swindled people out of their homes, but he'd also been part of this human-trafficking ring.

Lucas wanted to see him rot in jail.

But he sensed another person might be calling the shots.

"We know someone else in Tumbleweed is involved," Harrison said.

Stanley's eyes widened, his ruddy complexion going pale. "I wasn't involved," Stanley said. "At least not directly."

"Then how were you involved?" Lucas asked.

Stanley cut his eyes between them. "I need a lawyer, don't I?"

"You can ask for one if you want," Harrison said.

"But all deals stop when he shows up," Lucas said in

a harsh tone. "This ring has to be stopped. And if you take the fall, that's fine by me."

"No, no," Stanley shrieked. "I tell you I wasn't that involved."

Harrison folded his arms. "Then tell us what you know."

Stanley glanced down at his bony hands, which he kept twisting together. The man was pathetic. No way was he in charge of an organization like the men who'd abducted Charlotte's students.

But his silence had endangered countless innocent girls and Charlotte.

Lucas walked toward the door. "Either spill it or I'm throwing the book at you. And when I do, I'll make sure the media circulates the news that you talked."

Stanley lurched up from his seat, a muscle ticking in his narrow jaw. "You can't do that. They'll kill me."

Lucas shrugged. Harrison slammed his fist on the table, rattling the wood. "Then speak up. Because frankly I don't give a damn if they put your sorry butt in the ground."

"Not a damn," Lucas agreed flatly.

Stanley shoved his fingers through what was left of his thinning hair. "It wasn't me. But I was asked to set up some offshore accounts and I started asking questions."

Lucas returned to stand across from the man. "And you found out about the trafficking ring."

"Not at first," Stanley said, his voice shaky. "But eventually I kept asking and then got a cut to keep my mouth shut."

"Who paid you off?" Lucas asked.

"I don't know. The money—"

Lucas grabbed him by the collar and jerked him so hard the man's feet came off the floor. "I want a name."

"Geoffrey Williams," he shrieked. "He…paid me to keep quiet. He's head of the group in Tumbleweed. He…bought that last girl for himself."

Lucas's blood ran cold. He had gone to school with Geoffrey. Had admired the popular athlete.

But his name had cropped up when they'd been investigating his sister's disappearance. Lucas had remembered then that Geoffrey had pushed his little sister around.

Maybe he had a mean streak with women…

Geoffrey was also part of the town council. He purported to be helping the town, building the economy.

He'd even helped Honey get approval for the renovation of the homes she'd bought.

Dammit. How much of the money that he'd invested had come from sex trafficking?

AN HOUR LATER, Lucas and Harrison arrested Geoffrey Williams.

The cocky creep had no idea they suspected him, much less that Stanley had rolled on him.

He lawyered up immediately. But Lucas and Harrison had already obtained warrants for the man's house, business and personal computers. And the surveillance cameras at the ranch where Evie had been taken showed Williams paying for Evie, then discussing her future as his personal private sex slave.

Keenan also connected Williams to Louise—he had used a fake account to lure her into thinking he was a teenager interested in her. When he'd gotten her alone, though, she'd fought and he'd lost control and killed her.

He'd been furious and then began to look for another young girl to fill his needs. He'd stopped by Charlotte's studio to check on her business and spotted Evie.

Lucas escorted him to federal lockup and made certain that bail was not an option, and that he had no communication with anyone on the outside or in the jail. He didn't want the bastard to be released or call someone to come after Charlotte again.

Harrison left to go home to Honey, and Lucas drove by the hospital to pick up Charlotte. Evie was going to stay in the room with Adrian and Agnes for the night. The nurses had moved Mae Lynn in with them, hoping the four of them being reunited would help Mae Lynn in her recovery.

Charlotte was quiet as they drove back to his house. "I can go home now," she said, her voice soft, questioning.

"Yes, it should be safe."

"Good." She breathed out deeply. "Once I get the girls settled, I need to get my life in order."

Lucas didn't know what that meant, but he hoped to hell he was going to be part of that life.

Chapter Twenty-Five

Worry plagued Lucas as he drove Charlotte back to his cabin to retrieve her overnight bag, then to her house.

"The security company installed the alarm system," Lucas said, glad Brayden had taken care of meeting the company here and overseeing the installation.

"Let me show you how it works."

"Thanks." Nerves fluttered in her voice as he walked her inside and explained the system.

"I hope I can remember to use it and not trip it," Charlotte said.

"You'll get used to it, and you'll learn to appreciate it." He gently touched her shoulder. "I want you to be safe, Charlotte."

"You've been wonderful to me, Lucas," Charlotte said. "You're a man of your word. You found my students and brought them back. I can never repay you for that."

His throat thickened. "You don't owe me anything, Charlotte. It was my job."

Her smile faded. "Of course it was. The world is a better place because of it, too."

She pulled away and stiffened. "Thanks again."

Lucas sensed he'd said something wrong, but he

didn't know what it was. But he couldn't leave without telling her how he felt.

He took her hand in his, frowning when she tensed again.

"Charlotte, I know the case is over, but I have feelings for you. I want to see you again." God, he sounded awkward and stilted and should just tell her how much he loved her.

But something about her demeanor made him hesitate.

"You've done everything for me the last few days, and I appreciate it. But you have your life, and… I have to figure out how to live mine now."

"I don't care that you're blind," he said. "If you get your vision back, good, but if you don't, it won't matter to me."

"It matters to me." Her lips tightened into a thin line. "I'm not going to be a burden to anyone. And I certainly don't want your pity." She pulled her hand from his and turned to face her bedroom. "Now, please leave."

Panic caught in Lucas's throat. "That's not what this is," Lucas said. "I don't pity you, Charlotte. I admire the hell out of you. I know we can make it work."

"No, we can't," Charlotte said firmly. "Go home, Lucas. I…just want to be alone."

"But I love you," Lucas said in a rush.

A tense heartbeat passed, then Charlotte lifted her head as if she was looking at him. "We've only known each other for a few days, Lucas. Don't confuse protecting me with love. You did your job, now go home. I'm tired and want to go to bed."

Lucas studied her for a long moment. He loved her, wanted to be with her, to take care of her forever.

But she obviously didn't feel the same way.

He backed toward the door, his heart in his throat. "Call me if you need anything."

She nodded, but made no move to stop him as he closed the door.

CHARLOTTE CRIED HERSELF to sleep. Lucas had said he cared about her, wanted to be with her.

He'd even said he loved her.

She'd dreamed of having love all her life.

But she couldn't be with anyone until she knew how she was going to manage her life.

She refused to be a problem or burden to Lucas. If she gave into the feelings she had for him and allowed herself to rely on him, sooner or later he'd get tired of it.

Of her.

Then he'd resent her.

She couldn't bear that.

Needing to make a plan, she set the security system, then found her phone and called Rebecca. The vision-rehabilitation therapist had told her about a school for the blind.

Sure, she might get her vision back.

But she might not.

Until then, she couldn't rely on others. She would sign up for the school and take charge of her life.

She couldn't contemplate building a future with any-one until she took care of herself.

THE NEXT THREE weeks were excruciating for Lucas. He and Harrison and the other agents at the Bureau had made more arrests in the Shetland operation and had finally located and rescued the last of the original eleven missing girls.

Although they now believed that the real ringleader had escaped, information pointed to a plastic surgeon whom they suspected had given the man a new face.

That investigation was still on going.

He came inside from the horse stable and washed his hands.

He missed Charlotte like crazy.

But he wanted her to be happy so he'd left her alone.

Honey said that Charlotte had asked her to make some adjustments to her house to accommodate her lack of vision.

Meanwhile, his mother had taken steps to become a foster parent and Adrian, Agnes and Evie had moved in. Mae Lynn was making progress and would be moving in with them soon.

The house was bustling with the girls, who adored the horses and ranch life. His mother asked Dexter to buy each of them a horse to ride. In their spare time, he and his brothers were giving the girls riding lessons.

He'd just finished one with Evie. That girl was something else. She reminded him of Charlotte—all sweetness but full of spunk and fight.

His mother had a purpose now and seemed happier than he'd seen her in years. She'd revealed that she had a craft room where she worked with clay and had shown them her bust of Chrissy. He and his brothers had insisted she display it on the mantle near the dining table so Chrissy would be part of their family meals. No one at the table had been dry-eyed when they'd toasted Chrissy.

His mother had also opened up her craft room for the girls to paint.

He washed up from outside, then went to tell her good-night and found her in her craft room cleaning up.

"Thanks for giving the girls a riding lesson today," she said with a big smile. "They are so excited about being on the ranch."

Lucas hugged her. "You're incredible with them, Mom." She would have been incredible with his sister, too, but she'd been robbed of that.

"I enjoy having them on the ranch," she said with a smile. "This house has been quiet far too long. Besides, it's good practice for all the grandkids I hope to have."

"Harrison and Honey are working on it." They'd made the official announcement at the family dinner last night. His mother was thrilled.

He hadn't realized how much he wanted his own family until he'd watched his brother and Honey talk about their plans.

Charlotte would make a wonderful mother. If only she loved him...

His mother nudged him with a teasing grin. "You and Charlotte can add your own." Lucas clenched his hands by his sides, his gaze straying to the paintings the girls were doing.

"Lucas? You are in love with her, aren't you? I didn't misread the situation, did I?"

"No." He swallowed hard. "I told her I wanted to be with her, but she doesn't feel the same way."

A tense silence stretched between them, then his mother tugged his hand. "Come here for a minute, son. I want to show you something."

Lucas narrowed his eyes, but she led him to a side table, then lifted a cloth to reveal a clay piece.

"When Charlotte was here, I gave her some clay to work with. She was frustrated about everything, worried about the girls and missing her art." She moved the piece around to give him a better view. "Look at it, Lucas."

He studied the piece—it was a head. Deep eyes. A square chin.

"It's you, Lucas," she said softly. "It's the first clay piece she's ever done, and it's you." She wrapped her arm around his shoulder. "One look at the way she created your face, and I knew she was in love with you."

Lucas looked at her in disbelief, then studied the bust again. Was his mother right?

Could Charlotte possibly be in love with him?

THE LAST THREE weeks had been challenging for Charlotte.

"You look fabulous," Honey said as Charlotte seated herself in Honey's minivan.

"Thanks for picking me up."

"Are you kidding? I've missed you like crazy!"

Charlotte smiled. "I missed you, too."

But she was grateful for the education she'd received at the school for the blind. She still missed her sight, especially the colors and her artwork, but at least she'd learned to be independent, prepare her own meals and do daily household chores.

She would always need to rely on a driver and need help grocery shopping, but she would figure things out. Rebecca had recommended a service that would help with some of her needs so she didn't have to rely on friends or neighbors.

Honey started the engine and sped toward Tumbleweed.

"The girls are doing great," Honey said. "They love the ranch and can't stop talking about the riding lessons the men are giving them."

"I know. They wrote me letters about it," Charlotte said. "Mrs. Hawk was so generous to take them in."

"It's been good for her," Honey said. "She spent years grieving for Chrissy. Having these girls around and knowing that they need her has brought a real spark to her eyes."

Charlotte wanted to ask about Lucas, but she bit back the words. She missed him more and more each day. She just didn't know what to do about it.

And as much as she wanted to see the girls, visiting them at Hawk's Landing would be tough.

Although Lucas might have left town for another case by now...

Honey slowed then parked. "We're here. I'll go in and help you get settled if you want."

Charlotte hesitated. She'd missed her friend, but she didn't want to take advantage of Honey. And she had to prove to herself that she could manage on her own. "I can make it by myself, Honey. But thank you for everything."

Honey cut the engine and pulled Charlotte into a hug. "Listen to me, don't shut me out. I was your friend before all this happened, and I'll always be your friend."

Tears flooded Charlotte's eyes. Good grief. She'd thought she was past all the emotions.

"You'd still love me if I lost my sight, wouldn't you?" Honey asked.

Charlotte pulled back from her friend, Honey's words echoing in her ears. "Of course I would."

"Then don't push me away, because it won't work. You and I connected the first time we met. I've always wanted a sister, and I found her in you."

Charlotte squeezed Honey's hand. "I feel the same way. It's just—"

"I know you're independent and it's hard for you to accept help," Honey said. "It would be difficult for me, too. But I need you, Charlotte." Honey pulled Charlotte's hand over her belly, and Charlotte couldn't help but smile at her baby bump.

"Please say you'll be here for me and my son."

"A son?" Charlotte squeezed Honey's hands. "I bet Harrison and his mother are excited."

"They are. And I want you to be his godmother." Honey's voice softened. "Promise me you will."

How could she say no to that?

She promised she would, then hugged Honey again and allowed her to walk her to the door. Charlotte unlocked the door then Honey's footsteps echoed on the porch as she left.

Charlotte took a deep breath for courage and stepped inside.

A sweet aroma suffused her, and she paused inside the entryway. Someone had been in the house.

Maybe Honey had cleaned?

No, it wasn't cleaner she smelled. It was roses.

Soft music played in the background, then another scent—masculine, woodsy...

Her heart stuttered. "Lucas?"

"I'm here, Charlotte." Footsteps padded as he walked toward her. "I missed you."

Her heartache over him had intensified each day they'd been apart.

His hand brushed her cheek, then he took her hand in his and kneeled on the floor.

"I love you, Charlotte. I hope you don't mind the flowers, but I wanted to surprise you."

Love mushroomed inside her. "You did."

He slowly opened her palm, and she bit her bottom lip as she felt him place something inside.

"I'm not going away," he said. "I want to marry you and have a family with you."

She traced her fingers over the ring in her hand. An oval diamond, thin band with tiny stones inlaid in it. She imagined how it looked, but knew it didn't matter.

It was beautiful because Lucas was giving it to her.

His breath quickened as he closed his hands around hers. "I've dreamed about holding you and kissing you again every night." He brought her hands to his lips and kissed them. "Please say you want to be with me, too."

She clung to his hand, then kneeled in front of him. "I love you, too, Lucas." She looped her arms around his neck, then pressed a kiss to his lips. Her heart was bursting with happiness and love. "Yes, Lucas, I want to be your wife."

He swept her into a kiss that made her tremble Then he slipped the ring on her finger and kissed her again.

A kiss that promised that nothing would ever tear them apart.

Chapter Twenty-Six

"You look beautiful," Honey said, a note of wistfulness in her voice as she dabbed blush on Charlotte's cheeks.

"Thanks, Honey." She squeezed her friend's hand. "And thanks for helping me with my makeup."

"Not that you need anything," Honey said. "You have gorgeous skin."

Charlotte bit back that inner voice reminding her that it hadn't always been that way. She was grateful to the plastic surgeon who'd donated her time to repair Charlotte's birthmark at no cost.

Honey hesitated, and Charlotte imagined a tiny frown crinkling between her eyes. "Are you okay? Nervous?"

Charlotte shook her head. "No, sorry, sometimes the ghosts come back to haunt me."

Honey adjusted Charlotte's veil. "No ghosts today. Only happy thoughts."

"I am happy," Charlotte admitted. Even if she couldn't see her reflection in the mirror, she felt beautiful.

Lucas had given her that gift. As much as she wanted to see his face when she walked down the aisle, she'd learned to feel things with her other senses. She heard the love in his voice when he spoke to her, felt it in his touch, knew it in her heart.

"I wish I could see what you look like today," Charlotte said with a smile. "Your baby bump is growing."

"So are my boobs," Honey said with a laugh. "But Harrison doesn't seem to mind that."

They laughed together, then Honey took Charlotte's hand and she stood.

"Lucas is a lucky man," Honey said.

"I'm the lucky one."

Honey gently touched the end of Charlotte's hair, where she'd curled it around Charlotte's shoulders. "You're both lucky so don't sell yourself short, Charlotte. He needs you. I've seen it in his eyes. Those weeks you were gone, he was lost."

So was I.

But they'd found each other and she didn't intend to let go for a second.

Honey took her hand and guided her outside the big farmhouse. Giggles and whispers from the girls echoed in the background, blending with the guitar music. Finding out that Dexter played had been a surprise.

Having Adrian, Agnes, Evie and Mae Lynn, who was flourishing at Hawk's Landing, present was the icing on the cake.

"Deputy Bronson is here with Haley," Honey said. "I think they may be getting married next."

Charlotte smiled to herself. Since her hospital stay, she and Haley and Honey had become close friends. Rebecca, her vision therapist, had joined them for their weekly girls' night out.

The guitar music strummed softly in the background,

and Harrison's gruff voice whispered her name as he stepped up to walk her down the aisle.

"It's gorgeous here," Honey said. "The fall colors are in full bloom. We made an aisle for you with white chairs decorated in rose petals on the ground. Roses are everywhere, too, just like Lucas requested."

Roses reminded her of the night he'd proposed. Of the moment she realized she couldn't live without him.

"Lucas is a jittery mess," Harrison murmured as they started down the aisle. "He's still afraid he dreamed that you said yes."

A smile filled Charlotte's heart. Harrison walked slowly, careful to keep pace with her, but she could have walked the aisle by herself. Her pull to Lucas was that strong.

Harrison paused, and Charlotte inhaled Lucas's masculine scent. Lucas cradled her hand in his and she squeezed his, silently telling him how happy she was.

The reverend cleared his throat and began the ceremony.

His words faded though as she turned to face her groom. The power of Lucas's love bloomed deep within her, healing hurts and pains with its sweet intensity.

She not only felt safe at Hawk's Landing, but she also felt honored to have found this man.

Suddenly a quick pain flashed behind her eyes. Then light.

She tensed, dizzy for a second.

"Charlotte?" Lucas's concern resonated in his voice.

She blinked, then slowly colors began to slip into place. A sea of yellow, the moon, the reds and oranges of the leaves, the soft pinks of the roses, then… Lucas's face.

Lucas cupped her face between his hands. "Charlotte, honey, what's wrong?" She couldn't speak. She was mesmerized by the chiseled shape of his face, by his strong jaw, by the deep brown of his eyes as he looked into hers.

Time stood still. The wind sifted through the trees, creating its own music. Moonlight glimmered off his face.

"Charlotte, talk to me, honey," he murmured.

She lifted her hands and traced his jaw with her fingers. "I can see you, Lucas. I can see your eyes and that tiny scar on your forehead and that mouth that drives me wild."

A slow smile spread on Lucas's face as the truth dawned. Then he swept her in his arms and swung her around.

No one in the crowd understood what had happened yet, but they cheered and clapped.

Charlotte wrapped her arms around her husband and sealed their vows with a kiss.

Blue had always been her favorite color, but now brown had replaced it—the brown of Lucas's eyes because they were the color of love.

* * * * *

Look for the next book in USA TODAY
bestselling author Rita Herron's
BADGE OF JUSTICE *miniseries*
later in 2018.

And don't miss the previous title in the
BADGE OF JUSTICE *series:*

REDEMPTION AT HAWK'S LANDING

Available now from Harlequin Intrigue!

THE LIGHT WAS in her eyes, blinding her. Macey Night couldn't see past that too-bright light. She was strapped onto the operating-room table, but it wasn't the straps that held her immobile.

He'd drugged her.

"I could stare into your eyes forever." His rumbling voice came from behind the light. "So unusual, but then, you realize just how special you are, right, *Dr. Night*?"

She couldn't talk. He'd gagged her. They were in the basement of the hospital, in a wing that hadn't been used for years. Or at least, she'd thought it hadn't been used. She'd been wrong. About so many things.

"Red hair is always rare, but to find a redhead with heterochromia…it's like I hit the jackpot."

A tear leaked from her eye.

"Don't worry. I've made sure that you will feel everything that happens to you. I just—well, the drugs were to make sure that you wouldn't fight back. That's all. Not to impair the experience for you. Fighting back just ruins everything. I know what I'm talking about, believe me." He sighed. "I had a few patients early on— they were special like you. Well, not *quite* like you, but I think you get the idea. They fought and things got messy."

A whimper sounded behind her gag because he'd just taken his scalpel and cut her on the left arm, a long, slow slice from her inner wrist all the way up to her elbow.

"How was that?" he asked her. His voice was low, deep.

Nausea rolled in her stomach. Nausea from fear, from the drugs, from the absolute horror of realizing she'd been working with a monster and she hadn't even realized it. Day in and day out, he'd been at her side. She'd even thought about dating him. Thought about having *sex* with him. After all, Daniel Haddox was the most respected doctor at the hospital. At thirty-five, he'd already made a name for himself. He was *the* best surgeon at Hartford General Hospital, everyone said so.

He was also, apparently, a sadistic serial killer.

And she was his current victim.

All because I have two different-colored eyes. Two fucking different colors.

"I'll start slowly, just so you know what's going to happen." He'd moved around the table, going to her right side now. "I keep my slices light at first. I like to see how the patient reacts to the pain stimulus."

I'm not a patient! Nothing is wrong with me! Stop! Stop!

But he'd sliced her again. A mirror image of the wound he'd given her before, a slice on her right arm that began at her inner wrist and slid all the way up to her elbow.

"Later, the slices will get deeper. I have a gift with the scalpel, haven't you heard?" He laughed—it was a laugh that she knew too many women had found arousing. Dr. Haddox was attractive, with black hair and gleaming blue eyes. He had perfect white teeth, and the kind of easy, good-looking features that only aged well.

Doesn't matter what he looks like on the outside. He's a monster.

"Every time I work on a patient, I wonder…what is it like without the anesthesia?"

Sick freak.

"But not just any patient works for me. I need the special ones." He moved toward her face and she knew he was going to slice her again. He lifted the scalpel and pressed it to her cheek.

The fingers on her right hand jerked.

Wait—did I do that? Had her hand jerked just because of some reflex or were the drugs wearing off? He'd drugged her when she'd first walked into the basement with him. Then he'd undressed her, put her on the operating table and strapped her down. But before he could touch her any more, he'd been called away. The guy had gotten a text and rushed off—to surgery. To save a patient. She wasn't even sure how long he'd been gone. She'd been trapped on that operating table, staring up at the bright light the whole time he'd been gone. In her mind, she'd been screaming again and again for help that never came.

"You and I are going to have so much fun, and those beautiful eyes of yours will show me everything that you feel." He paused. "I'll be taking those eyes before I'm done."

Her right hand moved again. *She'd* made it move. The drugs he'd given her were wearing off. *His* mistake. She often responded in unusual ways to medicine. Hell, that was one of the reasons she'd gone into medicine in the first place. When she was six, she'd almost died after taking an over-the-counter children's pain medication. Her body processed medicines differently. She'd wanted to know why. Wanted to know how to predict who would have adverse reactions after she'd gone into cardiac arrest from a simple aspirin.

It's not just my eyes that are different. I'm different.

But her mother…her mother had been the main reason for her drive to enter the field of medicine. Macey had been forced to watch—helplessly—as cancer destroyed her beautiful mother. She'd wanted to make a change after her mother's death. She'd wanted to help people.

I never wanted to die like this!

But now she could move her left hand. Daniel wasn't paying any attention to her fingers, though. He was holding that scalpel right beneath her eye and staring down at her. She couldn't see his face. He was just a blur of dots—courtesy of that bright light.

She twisted her right hand and caught the edge of the strap. She began to slide her hand loose.

"The eyes will be last," he told her as if he'd just come to some major decision. "I've got to explore every inch of you to see why you're different. It's for the good of science. It's *always* for the good. For the betterment of mankind, a few have to suffer." He made a faint *hmm* sound. "Though I wonder about you…about us. With your mind…maybe…maybe we could have worked together."

And maybe he was insane. No, there wasn't any *maybe* about that. She'd gotten her right hand free, and her left was working diligently on the strap. Her legs were still secured, so she wasn't going to be able to just jump off the table. Macey wasn't even sure if her legs would hold her. The drug was still in her body, but it was fading fast.

"But you aren't like that, are you, Dr. Night?" Now his voice had turned hard. "I watched you. Followed you. Kept my gaze on you when you thought no one was looking."

She'd felt hunted for days, for weeks, but she'd tried to tell herself she was just being silly. She worked a lot, and the stress of the job had been making her imagine things. She was in her final few weeks of residency work, and everyone knew those hours were killer.

Only in her case, they literally were.

"You don't get that we can't always save every patient. Sometimes, the patients die and it is a learning experience for everyone."

Bullshit. He was just trying to justify his insanity.

"You see things in black-and-white. They're not like that, though. The world is full of gray." He moved the scalpel away from her cheek...only to slice into her shoulder. "And red. Lots and lots of red—"

She grabbed the scalpel from him. Because he wasn't expecting her attack, she ripped it right from his fingers, and then she shoved it into his chest as deep and as hard as she could.

Daniel staggered back. Macey shot up, then nearly fell off the table because her legs were still strapped and her body was shaking. She yanked at the straps, jerking frantically against them as she heard him moaning on the floor.

The straps gave way. She sprang off the table and immediately collapsed. She fell onto Daniel—and the weight of her body drove the scalpel even deeper into him.

"You…bitch…"

"You bastard," she whispered right back. Then she was heaving off him. Her blood was dripping from her wounds and she crawled to the door. He grabbed her ankle, but she kicked back, slamming her foot into his face, and Macey heard the satisfying crunch as she broke his nose.

He wasn't so perfect any longer.

"Macey!"

She yanked open the door. Her legs felt stronger. Or maybe adrenaline was just making her stronger. She ran out of the small room and down the hallway. He was going to come after her. She knew it. She needed help. She needed it *fast*. There were no security monitors on that hallway. No cameras to watch her. No help for her.

Her breath heaved out and her blood splattered onto the floor. She didn't look back, too terrified that she'd see Daniel closing in on her. The elevator was up ahead. She hit the button, smearing it with her blood. She waited and waited and—

Ding. The doors slid open. She fell inside and whipped around.

Daniel was coming after her. He still had the scalpel in his chest. *Because he's a freaking doctor. He knows that if he pulls it out, he's done. He'll have massive blood loss right away. But the longer that scalpel stays in…*

It gave him the chance to come for her.

His lips were twisted in a snarl as he lunged for the doors.

She slapped the button to close the elevator, again and again and again, and the doors *closed*.

Macey was shaking, crying, bleeding. But she'd gotten away. The elevator began to move. Gentle instrumental music filled the air.

The doors opened again, spitting her out on the lobby level. She heard the din of voices, phones ringing and a baby crying somewhere in the distance. She walked out of the elevator, naked and bloody.

Silence. Everything just stopped as she staggered down the corridor.

"H-help me..."

A wide-eyed nurse rose from the check-in desk. "Dr. Night?"

Macey looked down at her bloody body. *"H-help me..."*

"I'VE FOUND HIM." Macey Night exhaled slowly as she faced her team at the FBI headquarters in Washington, DC. All eyes were on her, and she knew just how important this meeting was. She'd spent five years hunting, searching, never giving up, and now, finally "I believe that I know the location of Daniel Haddox." She cleared her throat and let her gaze drift around the conference room table. "Daniel...the serial killer otherwise known as 'The Doctor' thanks to the media."

A low whistle came from her right—from FBI special agent Bowen Murphy. "I thought he was dead."

Macey had wanted him to be dead. "I never believed that he died from his injuries. That was just a story that circulated in the news. Daniel was the best surgeon I ever met. He knew how to survive."

"And how to vanish," said Samantha Dark. Samantha Dark was in charge of their team. The group had been her brainchild. Samantha had hand selected every member of their unit. The FBI didn't have official profilers—actually, "profiler" wasn't even a title that they used. Instead, Samantha and her team were called "behavioral analysis experts." But the people in that conference room were different from the BAU members who worked typical cases in the violent crimes division.

Each person in that small conference room—each person there—had an intimate connection to a serial killer.

Her gaze slid over her team members.

Samantha Dark…so fragile in appearance with her pale skin, dark hair and delicate build, but so strong inside. Samantha's lover had been a killer, but she had brought him down. She'd been the one to realize that personal connections to serial perpetrators weren't a weakness…they could be a strength.

Tucker Frost. The FBI agent's bright blue stare held Macey's. Tucker's brother had been a serial killer. The infamous Iceman who'd taken too many victims in New Orleans. His exploits were legendary—scary stories that children whispered late at night.

Her hands fisted as her gaze slid to the next member of their team. Bowen Murphy. His blond hair was disheveled, and his dark gaze was intense as it rested upon her. Bowen had hunted down a serial killer, a man who the local authorities had sworn didn't exist. But Bowen had known the perp was out there. A civilian, he'd gone on the hunt and killed the monster in the shadows.

And then…then there was Macey herself. She'd worked side by side with a serial killer. She'd been his victim. She'd been the only "patient" to escape his care alive.

Now she'd found him. After five years of always looking over her shoulder and wondering if he'd come for her again. She'd. Found. Him. "You're right, Samantha," Macey acknowledged with a tilt of her head. "Daniel Haddox *did* know how to vanish." Her voice was quiet. Flat. "But I knew he wouldn't turn away from medicine. I knew he would have to return to his patients. He would *have* to pick up a scalpel again." But there had been so many places he could have gone. He could have easily stayed under the radar, opening up a clinic that dealt only in cash. One that didn't have any government oversight because it wasn't legitimate. One that catered to the poorest of communities.

Where he would have even greater control over his victims.

"I also knew that he wouldn't stop killing," Macey said. Once more, her gaze slid back to Bowen. She often found herself doing that—looking to Bowen. She wasn't even sure why, not really. They'd been partners on a few cases, but...

His gaze held hers. Bowen looked angry. That was odd. Bowen usually controlled his emotions so well. It was often hard to figure out just what the guy was truly thinking. He would present a relaxed, casual front to the world, but beneath the surface, he could be boiling with intensity.

"Why didn't you tell me that you were hunting him?" Bowen's words were rough, rumbling. He had a deep voice, strong, and she sucked in a breath as she realized that his anger was fully directed at *her*.

"The Doctor isn't an active case for our group," Macey said. They had more than enough current crimes to keep them busy. "We have other killers that we have been hunting and I didn't want to distract from—"

"Bullshit." His voice had turned into a rasp. "You

forgot you were on a team, Macey. What impacts you impacts us all."

She licked her lips. He was right. Her news *did* impact them all. "That's why I called this meeting. Why I am talking to you all now." Even though her instincts had screamed for her to act. For her to race up to the small town of Hiddlewood, North Carolina, and confront the man she believed to be Daniel Haddox. But... "I want backup on this case." Because the dark truth was that Macey didn't trust herself to face Daniel alone.

Samantha's fingers tapped on the table. "How can you be so sure you've found him?"

Macey fumbled a bit and hit her laptop. Immediately, her files projected onto the screen to the right. "This victim was discovered twenty-four hours ago." Her words came a little too fast, so she sucked in another breath, trying to slow herself down. "A victim who is currently in the Hiddlewood ME's office. The autopsy hasn't even begun, but the medical examiner was struck by what she felt was a ritualistic pattern on the victim." She licked her lips. "Look at the victim's arms. The slices, from wrist to elbow. The Doctor always made those marks first on his victims. Those are his test wounds. He makes them to be sure his victims can feel the pain of their injuries, but still not fight him."

Silence. Macey clasped her hands together. "We got lucky on this one because we have a medical examiner who pays close attention to detail—and who seems very familiar with the work of Daniel Haddox. Dr. Sofia Lopez sent those files to the FBI, and I've got... I've got a friend here who knows what I've been looking for in terms of victim pathology." When she'd seen those wounds, Macey had known she'd found the bastard who'd tormented her. "I think the man who killed this victim is Daniel Haddox, and I think we need to get a team up to Hiddlewood right away."

Tucker leaned forward, narrowing his eyes as he stared at the screen. "You think this perp will kill again? You're so sure we're not dealing with some copycat who just heard about Daniel Haddox's crimes and thought he could imitate the murders?" Tucker pressed.

No, she wasn't sure. How could she be? "I think we need to get up there." Her hands twisted in front of her. She wasn't supposed to let cases get personal, Macey knew that, but...how could this case *not* be personal? Haddox had marked her, literally. He'd changed her whole life. She'd left medicine. She'd joined the FBI. She'd hunted killers because...

Because deep down, I'm always hunting him. The one who got away. The one I have to stop.

Samantha stared at her in silence for a moment. A far-too-long moment. Macey realized she was holding her breath. And then—

"Get on a plane and get up there," Samantha directed curtly. Then she pointed to Bowen. "You, too, Bowen. I want you and Macey working together on this one. Get up there, take a look at the crime scene, and..." Her gaze cut back to Macey. "You work with the ME. If Daniel Haddox really committed this homicide, then you'll know. You know his work better than anyone."

Because she still carried his "work" on her body. And in her mind. In the dark chambers that she fought so hard to keep closed.

But now I've found you, Daniel. You won't get away again.

Tucker rose and came around the table toward her

as she fumbled with her laptop. "Macey…" His voice was pitched low so that only she could hear him. "Are you sure you want to be the one going after him? Believe me on this…sometimes confronting the demons from your past doesn't free you. It just pulls you deeper into the darkness."

Her hands stilled on her laptop. She looked into Tucker's eyes and saw the sympathy that filled his stare. If anyone would know about darkness, it would be Tucker. She lifted her chin, hoping she looked confident. "I want to put this particular darkness in a cell and make sure he *never* gets out."

He nodded, but the heaviness never left his expression. "If you and Bowen hit trouble, call in the rest of the team, got it? We always watch out for each other."

Yes, they did.

She put her laptop into her bag. Tucker filed out of the room, but Samantha lingered near the doorway. Bowen wasn't anywhere to be seen. Macey figured that he must have slipped away while she was talking to Tucker. Clutching her bag, she headed toward Samantha.

"How many victims do you think he's claimed?" Samantha's voice was quiet as she asked the question that haunted Macey.

Every single night…when she wondered where Daniel was…when she wondered if he had another patient trapped on his table. *How many?* "We know he killed five patients before he took me." They'd found their remains in that hospital, hidden behind a makeshift wall in the basement. Daniel had made his own crypt for those poor people. He'd killed them, and then he'd sealed them away.

"He's been missing for several years," Macey continued. Her heart drummed too fast in her chest.

"And serial killers don't just stop, not cold turkey." Samantha tilted her head as she studied Macey. "He might have experienced a cooling-off period, but he wouldn't have been able to give up committing the murders. He would have needed the rush that he got when he took a life."

How many victims? "I don't know how many," Macey whispered. And, because she trusted Samantha, because Samantha was more than just her boss—she was her friend—Macey said, "I'm afraid to find out."

Because every one of those victims would be on *her*. After all, Macey was the one who hadn't stopped him. She'd run away from him, so terrified, and when she'd fled, he'd escaped.

And lived to kill another day.

Samantha's hand rose and she squeezed Macey's shoulder. "You didn't hurt those people—*none* of those people."

"I ran away." She licked her lips.

"You survived. You were a victim then. That's what you were supposed to do—*survive*."

She wasn't a victim any longer. "I'm an FBI agent now."

"Yes." Samantha held her gaze. "And he won't get away again."

No, he damn well wouldn't.

After a quick planning talk with Samantha, Macey slipped into the hallway and hurried toward her small office. As always, their floor was busy, a hum of activity, and she could hear the rise and fall of voices in the background. She kept her head down and soon she was in her office, shutting that door behind her—

"I would have helped you."

Macey sucked in a sharp breath. Bowen stood next to the sole window in the small room, his gaze on the city below. His hands were clasped behind his back, and she could see the bulk of his weapon and holster beneath the suit jacket he wore.

She put her laptop down on the desk. "Samantha said we should be ready to fly in an hour. She's giving us the FBI's jet to use—"

He turned toward her. "Do you trust me, Mace?"

Mace. That was the nickname he'd adopted for her, and half the time, she wasn't even sure that he realized he was changing her name. But…it was softer when he said "Mace" and not "Macey." For some reason, she usually felt good when he used that nickname.

She didn't feel good right then. *Do you trust me?* Was that a trick question? She frowned at him. "You're my partner. I have to trust you." Or else they'd both be screwed. She was supposed to watch his back, and he was supposed to watch hers. It was pretty much the only way the FBI worked.

He crossed his arms over his chest as he considered her. "I have to ask… What will happen if you come face-to-face with Daniel Haddox?"

She stared up at him, but for a moment, she didn't see Bowen. She saw Daniel. Smiling. His eyes gleaming. And a scalpel in his hand. The scalpel was covered in her blood.

Don't miss
INTO THE NIGHT
available December 2017
wherever HQN Books and ebooks are sold.

www.Harlequin.com

COMING NEXT MONTH FROM

ⓗ HARLEQUIN®

I N T R I G U E

Available January 16, 2018

#1761 OUT OF THE DARKNESS
The Finnegan Connection • by Heather Graham
High school sweethearts Sarah Hampton and Tyler Grant had their romance torn apart by a massacre. But now that they have a second chance, the horrors of their past prove to be closer than they ever imagined.

#1762 LAWMAN FROM HER PAST
Blue River Ranch • by Delores Fossen
Deputy Cameron Doran thought he'd seen the last of his ex, Lauren Beckett. But when she shows up on his ranch after a home invasion and with a shocking story about his nephew, he's not about to turn his back on her.

#1763 SECURED BY THE SEAL
Red, White and Built • by Carol Ericson
Britt Jansen will do anything to find her sister—including going undercover in the Russian mob, where she teams up with navy SEAL sniper Alexei Ivanov. But can she trust her secret with a man whose eyes are set on stone-cold revenge?

#1764 RANGER DEFENDER
Texas Brothers of Company B • by Angi Morgan
Texas Ranger Slate Thompson may be the only person who believes what Vivian Watts has been saying all this time—that her brother is innocent. But can he face down his own when evidence begins to point to police corruption in the case?

#1765 MISSING IN BLUE MESA
The Ranger Brigade: Family Secrets • by Cindi Myers
Michelle Munson has infiltrated a cult in order to uncover the truth about her sister's death. But when her baby is kidnapped, she knows she's in over her head. Ranger Ethan Reynolds may be her last hope in the Colorado wilderness.

#1766 LOVING BABY
The Protectors of Riker County • by Tyler Anne Snell
Chief Deputy Suzy Simmons isn't impressed by millionaire James Callahan's killer body or bulletproof charm. But when he draws her into an investigation involving a missing baby, she wonders why the man who has everything has taken on the case.

YOU CAN FIND MORE INFORMATION ON UPCOMING HARLEQUIN® TITLES, FREE EXCERPTS AND MORE AT WWW.HARLEQUIN.COM.

HICNM0118

SPECIAL EXCERPT FROM

H HARLEQUIN®

INTRIGUE

Sarah Hampton knows that the recent murder of an old friend is linked to a terrifying night they experienced back in high school, and war-hardened Tyler Grant is the only one who knows the danger they're in...

Read on for a sneak preview of
OUT OF THE DARKNESS
by Heather Graham

Tyler watched as she walked into the parlor. Sarah. Whom he hadn't seen in a decade. She hadn't changed at all. Yet she had changed incredibly. There was nothing of the child left to her. Her facial lines had sharpened into beautiful detail. She had matured naturally and beautifully; all the little soft edges of extreme youth had fallen away to leave an elegantly cast blue-eyed beauty there as if a picture had come into sharp focus. She was wearing her hair at shoulder length; it had darkened a little into a deep, sun-touched honey color.

He stood. She was staring at him in turn.

Seeing what kind of a difference the years had made.

"Hey," he said softly.

They were both awkward, to say the least. She started to move forward quickly—the natural inclination to hug someone you held dear and hadn't seen in a long time.

He did the same.

She stopped.

He stopped.

Then they both smiled and laughed, and she stepped forward into his arms.

Holding her again, he knew why nothing else had ever worked for him. He'd met so many women—many of them bright, beautiful and wonderful—yet nothing had ever become more than brief moments of enjoyment, of gentle caring. Never this…connection.

He had to remember she had only called on him because their friend had been killed, and he was the only one who could really understand just what it was like.

They drew apart. It felt as if the clean scent of her shampoo and the delicate, haunting allure of her fragrance lingered, a sweet and poignant memory all around him.

"You came," she said. "Thanks. I know this is crazy, but…Hannah. To have survived what happened that October, and then…have this happen. I understand you're some kind of law enforcement now."

"No. Private investigator. That's why I'm not so sure how I can really be of any help here."

"Private investigators get to investigate, right?" Sarah asked.

When the horror of their past is resurrected, can Tyler keep Sarah safe from a killer set on finishing what he started?

OUT OF THE DARKNESS *by* New York Times *bestselling author Heather Graham.*

Available January 16, 2018 from Harlequin® Intrigue.

www.Harlequin.com

HIEXP0118

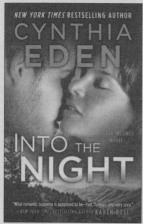

$7.99 U.S./$9.99 CAN.

EXCLUSIVE
Limited Time Offer

$1.⁰⁰ OFF

New York Times Bestselling Author
CYNTHIA EDEN

returns with a gripping
Killer Instinct novel

INTO THE
NIGHT

Available December 26, 2017.
Pick up your copy today!

HQN™

$1.⁰⁰ OFF
the purchase price of
INTO THE NIGHT by Cynthia Eden.

Offer valid from December 26, 2017, to January 31, 2018.
Redeemable at participating retail outlets. Not redeemable at Barnes & Noble.
Limit one coupon per purchase. Valid in the U.S.A. and Canada only.

52615333

Canadian Retailers: Harlequin Enterprises Limited will pay the face value of this coupon plus 10.25¢ if submitted by customer for this product only. Any other use constitutes fraud. Coupon is nonassignable. Void if taxed, prohibited or restricted by law. Consumer must pay any government taxes. Void if copied. Inmar Promotional Services ("IPS") customers submit coupons and proof of sales to Harlequin Enterprises Limited, PO Box 31000, Scarborough, ON M1R 0E7, Canada. Non-IPS retailer—for reimbursement submit coupons and proof of sales directly to Harlequin Enterprises Limited, Retail Marketing Department, 225 Duncan Mill Rd., Don Mills, ON M3B 3K9, Canada.

U.S. Retailers: Harlequin Enterprises Limited will pay the face value of this coupon plus 8¢ if submitted by customer for this product only. Any other use constitutes fraud. Coupon is nonassignable. Void if taxed, prohibited or restricted by law. Consumer must pay any government taxes. Void if copied. For reimbursement submit coupons and proof of sales directly to Harlequin Enterprises, Ltd 482, NCH Marketing Services, P.O. Box 880001, El Paso, TX 88588-0001, U.S.A. Cash value 1/100 cents.

5 65373 00076 2   (8100)0 12326

® and ™ are trademarks owned and used by the trademark owner and/or its licensee.

© 2017 Harlequin Enterprises Limited

PHCOUPCEHI0118